# Lazlo Strangolov's

## feather and Bone

ghost writing from the underground

**WALKER
BOOKS**

546398

This novel is dedicated
to the chickens

And the third angel sounded, and there fell a great star from heaven, burning as it were a lamp, and it fell upon the third part of the rivers, and upon the fountains of waters.

Book of Revelation 8:10

# Foreword by Matt Whyman

The book in your hands is a curious discovery. It has been penned by an author with a life story as odd and compelling as the tale to follow. That he has entrusted me to introduce it is a great pleasure and a crying shame. Why? Because I know for sure that he will never emerge from his world to present it himself.

Lazlo Strangolov isn't just a recluse. This is an individual who has gone to earth in every way. All I can say is that he has yet to see daylight this century. The man is free to leave his underground bunker, and at times I have wondered whether embarrassment keeps him down there as much as his fears. For on closing the hatch, on 31 December 1999,

Strangolov was convinced that the dawn of the new millennium would mark the end of the world.

I knew Lazlo briefly as a boy. We grew up on the same street, only to lose contact when his father moved the family back to his native village on the Romanian–Hungarian border (a region better known as Transylvania). At the time, in the eighties, the threat of nuclear war was very real. Mister Strangolov, a God-fearing and domineering individual at the end of a long-term posting as a translator at the Romanian Embassy, grew more unsettled than most by the issue. According to neighbours, the poor man eventually suffered some kind of psychological breakdown. One night, he loaded his wife and son into a taxi for the station, telling the driver they would be travelling by rail, ferry, coach and then horse-drawn carriage to reach their destination.

As for Lazlo, I remember him to be a pale and superstitious lad prone to headaches, particular about the shine of his shoes and picky about his food. Despite this, he possessed a rich imagination and an accent that led to bigger kids making Dracula jokes at his expense. Looking back, he did little to dispel the rumours about why the street lamp outside his family home always flickered through each night.

On the rare occasion that he stole outside, Lazlo would suggest that we hang out at the church cemetery. There, we'd conjure up yarns from reading ancient gravestone inscriptions and he would spook me with claims that he could see malevolent spirits. Three decades ago, this opened my eyes to the power and impact of a good story. It might even have steered me towards becoming a writer in my own right.

In fact, it is my work as a novelist that prompted Lazlo to contact me. Last year, out of nowhere, I received an email in which he politely enquired whether I might read a literary effort of his own. Lazlo made no mention of his whereabouts or what he had done with his life in all the years since we lost touch. Intrigued, I invited him to send me something. Lazlo responded by suggesting that he would prefer it if I travelled to him, and provided a deeply unconventional address. It was, quite simply, co-ordinates on a map. I have been sworn not to disclose the precise details, but it persuaded me to print out the e-ticket he supplied and catch a budget flight to a rural location in Eastern Europe, deep within the Carpathian Mountains. There, quite literally, I came to drop into the self-contained world of my old friend.

The apocalypse may not have taken place, yet Lazlo remains convinced that it *will* occur. He has inherited a paranoid, visionary spirit from his father, and fuelled it through extensive research. His bunker is wired up to the Web, protected by custom-built firewalls, and powered like his heat and lighting by an internal generator. Lazlo also has an unidentified "watcher" on the outside who ensures that he remains safe, fed and well. Life underground has clearly taken its toll, however. He is stooped and gaunt, with shadow pools for cheeks, pale eyes and bone-white skin to match his hair. We may have been born in the same year, but time appears to have ticked faster for one of us.

Then again, if Lazlo is correct in his recalculations, none of us have long left on this earth. At least not those who choose to ignore his warnings. He would not tell me how or when the unprepared would meet their doom. When I pressed him, he produced a handwritten manuscript, thick with scribbles in the margins, and said the answers were hidden within. All that any reader required, so he assured me, was a sharp eye, an open mind and an ability to read between the lines. Those who worked it out, he said, would learn the nature of the catastrophe we face, as well as the exact date this coming summer on which it would occur. Those smart enough to get it right, he disclosed, would at least have a chance to protect themselves and survive.

With no wish to appear rude by dismissing such claims out of hand, I asked if I might read the opening chapters of the manuscript. Lazlo invited me to make myself comfortable in his subterranean library while he brewed a pot of nettle leaf tea. I didn't notice when he set the cup beside me. The truth is I became so spellbound by the story that some hours later, on reaching the final page, I had to remind myself to blink.

I can confirm that a date is buried in the text. Watch out for two clues, as well as a reference to the cataclysmic event from the Bible's Book of Revelation that is said to mark the beginning of the End Times. It is not my place to tell you whether we should believe Lazlo and take steps to prepare for the worst. All I can say is that the author regards it as being of the utmost importance. Indeed, his decision to write the manuscript by hand, rather than computer, was driven by a fear that hackers might uncover his prophecies before he felt ready to go public. At worst, as he told me, they might sell the information to sinister forces determined to suppress it.

After much persuasion, Lazlo allowed me to leave with the manuscript. He made me swear not to let it out of my sight, and to seek a publisher who would also undertake to protect his whereabouts. I've done everything I can to keep his ongoing anxieties at bay. On occasion, I've had to remind myself that I'm dealing with a man who has lived a very sheltered life indeed.

Understandably, for someone sold on the idea that bad times are ahead, Lazlo is extremely concerned that his message is not lost in translation from manuscript to final book. This means that every morning I switch on my computer to find a string of emails have come in from him overnight. He has queried every step of the publishing process, and insisted that even his scribblings are reproduced in the finished pages.

I am sure he won't mind me telling you, this is one high-maintenance author.

Once, under pressure from Lazlo to promise not to move a single comma, I lost the plot and told him his secret code was "the kind of thing crackpots shout at bins in back alleys". I saw sense straight away, apologizing profusely and stressing how much I just wanted the story itself to reach an audience. After a fortnight's silence, Lazlo saw fit to forgive me. The episode made me realize how easily I could have caused him to withdraw the book from publication. Since then, I have taped a note to my computer monitor that simply reads, *Stay calm.*

And so, having learned the value of patience, no matter how badly tested, I can at last place you

in the trust of a true ghost writer from the underground. All I ask is that you take a deep breath and
prepare for…

# feather and Bone

**Matt Whyman,**
**with permission from the author.**

# Lazlo Strangolov's feather and Bone

# 1

My father once walked our dog into these woods, and never came home again. A little later than normal, she appeared at the garden gate without him. I cannot tell you any more. This is because every time my mother recounts the tale, her words fall away just as soon as she begins. Then the tears take over.

"He was a good man," she will struggle to finish. "A good man who chose the wrong path."

Now, it is my duty to walk the dog. Solace is white as a snowdrop, with a long muzzle, arching ears, and eyes that are impossible to fathom. There is some wolf in her, from the tips of her teeth to her loping stride, but I feel safe with such a presence at my side. For the woods fan out from where I live, in a small community nestled in the cleft of a steep mountain slope. This means I have no choice but to head for the trees to exercise her, and it isn't always a tranquil place to be.

In springtime, when the violets emerge under the canopy, I could spend all day there. Walking the old deer tracks, I can see dragonflies flitting through sunbeams and hear woodpeckers hard at work. I wish the flowers would last all year round. For as soon as they begin to wither and fade, I can't help thinking that eventually the same thing happens to us all.

Towards late autumn, when all the leaves lie rotting on the ground, the woods spend more time in darkness than light. Solace still has to be walked, however. First thing in the morning and again before bed. It means throughout the winter months I leave our cottage with a lurch in my heart, and pray my head torch won't burn out before I am safely back.

The torch belonged to my father. It is an invention of his, in fact, and one of many he cobbled together in his workshop. Instead of being powered by batteries, which are so hard to come by out here, I simply slot the device onto two prongs mounted on top of a tin box. By winding a handle at the side for a minute or so, the element inside the torch flickers into life and then builds to a steady glow. As soon as I remove it from the prongs, I can count on thirty minutes of light at most before the charge within expires. Once I've strapped it tight around my ears, and wrapped up against the cold outside, I try to leave the house without disturbing my mother. I am not always successful.

On the way out this time, she floats down the staircase, as pale as ever, and offers me a grateful smile for taking care of Solace. Even so, nothing can disguise the fact that she's looking at me as if we might never see each other again.

"I'll be OK," I tell her. "Remember what he used to say?"

My mother knows the answer very well. Whenever I awoke with nightmares as a little boy, she used to hover at the bedroom door while my father assured me that all would be well.

"He would ask you to guess what he feared the most."

"It wasn't vampire bats, werewolves or grave robbers," I say. "He'd simply go on shaking his head until I ran out of things that frightened me."

"And then," my mother reminds me with absolute conviction, "he would tell you he was scared of *nothing*."

As a pack animal, Solace looks to me for guidance and authority. This isn't so easy when you're as slight in build as I am. My name is Kamil, which means

5

"perfect" in this region, but I am far from that. I shall be twelve years old next birthday, and yet most people mark me down as being two years younger. I also wish that my voice would hurry up and break. For when my dog senses a presence in the meadow between our community and the woods, my appeals for her to return sound weedy, shrill and even desperate.

"Come back, Solace. Come *here*!"

This evening, she shoots from my side before we've even reached the tree line. A waning moon hangs over the woods, skewed to one side as if knocked from a fixing. What little light it provides is just enough to determine where the night sky meets the earth.

"Hey, Kamil! Keep your dog under control!" I recognize the voice before I find the figure in the torch beam, and feel only relief. It's Flori, the poacher's daughter. People say Flori has the look of a doe and the instinct of a fox. Sure enough, when she shrinks from Solace I note all the wire for her snares looped over her shoulder.

"Don't be afraid," I say. "Her bark is worse than her bite."

"I would prefer not to be at the wrong end of either," she replies. "Where are you going at this hour?"

"Solace needs her exercise," I say. "You can't keep a dog like this shut in all day."

"But every living creature will go to ground," she protests, coming closer now. Flori is wearing a camouflage coat and a woollen cap pulled low over her brow. It makes the hair splayed over her ears look more like feathers. "Thanks to Solace," she continues, "all the rabbits in this meadow must be safely in their burrows by now. They can sense a predator far quicker than you or I."

"Then come with me," I suggest, thinking of the company. "And bring your traps."

Flori seems to stiffen at this, and I know just what she's thinking.

"But nobody goes into the woods after dark."

"I do."

"You have no choice. You have Solace."

"Are you frightened?" Flori is only a few months older than me, but easily a foot taller, so I face up to her directly now and cross my fingers behind my back. "*I'm* not scared of anything."

flori

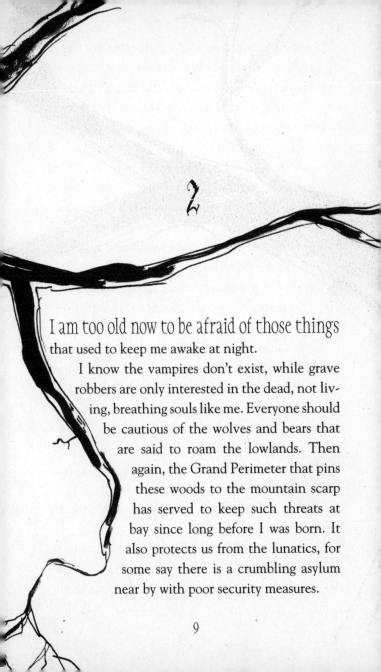

## 2

I am too old now to be afraid of those things that used to keep me awake at night.

I know the vampires don't exist, while grave robbers are only interested in the dead, not living, breathing souls like me. Everyone should be cautious of the wolves and bears that are said to roam the lowlands. Then again, the Grand Perimeter that pins these woods to the mountain scarp has served to keep such threats at bay since long before I was born. It also protects us from the lunatics, for some say there is a crumbling asylum near by with poor security measures.

After dark, out here, what troubles me is a fear of the unknown. Unless I ever discover what happened to my father, I shall always carry the thought that the same fate might befall me. I am constantly prepared to come across his remains, of course. If the worst occurred to him, then nature must have made use of his body by now. The rooks would have squabbled over his eyes, leaving the flies and the scavengers to take care of his flesh. And slowly, like the flowers, he would have returned to the earth. Even so, I sometimes wonder if perhaps I might find his bones if I just wander from the path.

By day, I'm too scared to look in case I find something. By night, I'm more frightened that something might find *me*.

In my mind, whatever it is that claimed my father must be hungry for more by now. That's why I'm so relieved that Flori has joined me as we push through the low-hanging branches where the path divides the trees. Leaving the meadow behind us, we face a different brand of darkness altogether.

"How far shall we go?" she asks, walking close beside me.

"To the Squawk Box," I say. "I always see rabbits there."

Flori doesn't reply. She knows the place I have in mind, and for a minute we simply follow the tunnel of light from my head torch. It picks out all the turns and textures in the path, the exposed roots and splintered sticks, as well as puddles formed by cloven hoof prints. Every now and then, Solace passes through the beam. The one time she turns to check on us, her eyes burn like match-heads. For a second, with the shadow of her ears thrown far ahead, she looks like a dog transformed into a demon. But I am not afraid of Solace. It is what I *can't* see that unnerves me. The sense that something off the path is aware of our presence.

"If my father knew I had come into the woods at this hour," breathes Flori, "I don't know if he'd be proud or mad at me."

"Do you want to follow in his footsteps?" I ask. "Your dad knows everything about setting traps. He's a master."

"What he does best is work without leaving a trace. Nobody has ever caught him, and every day there's something cooking in the pot."

"You're lucky," I say. "All I do is eat from tins and jars and cartons."

"It's just the way it is. We live in lean times, Kamil. How long has it been now?"

"A year and two months," I say. "The gates to the Squawk Box closed the same week that my father disappeared."

I reflect on what I have said as we continue on our way. All is quiet right now, and very still. Should

11

a breeze get up, I think to myself, then the upper branches will start to clash and Flori might lose her nerve. For her sake, I am careful not to look away from the path. If I swing the torch beam through the trees that flank us, it's easy to see things that aren't really there. At least that's what I have to tell myself, because there is a time on every walk when Solace bolts into the undergrowth, as she does right now. She's picked up on a presence near by. Most

12

likely it's a squirrel or a hare. Even so, the noise of the pursuit, from the snapping twigs to the violent shuddering of bushes, leaves my heart in my mouth.

"I don't like this," says Flori. She follows the beam from my head torch as I chase the commotion, but all I do is turn full circle. "Should we leave her here?"

"Just a moment longer," I say. "Solace will never abandon us."

"We really should walk on," insists Flori, with some urgency in her voice.

I look around one more time, seeking to glimpse my dog as the light jumps from trunk to trunk, only for Solace to slink up behind us. I find her with a start, looking strangely cowed. Alarmingly, the rustle and twang of branches does not stop with her appearance. It continues for a matter of seconds, encircling us, it seems: the sound of something far bigger than a squirrel and swifter than a hare, which then breaks away into the darkness.

Flori and I exchange a glance. "A deer," I say. "It has to be."

"But there *are* no more deer in these woods," she replies, wide-eyed as she faces me. "The Grand Perimeter doesn't just keep the wolves and bears and lunatics away, Kamil."

I know that she is right, though it does little to

reassure me. The Grand Perimeter is as high as some of the trees and finished with coils of barbed wire. I sometimes think the only way in would be with wings.

"We don't have far to go now," I assure her, and remind myself to stay calm. "If we cut short the walk our fears will only chase us home."

I cannot tell you when the Squawk Box first opened for business. Nobody around here really knows. Some say she is older than the community itself. They claim Mister Petri's forefathers built the Grand Perimeter first, followed by the cottages to house the first workers. Before the gates closed for the final time, I often wondered what was first needed to begin a big industrial poultry farm like this one. Did they pack out the roosts with countless chickens or start by hatching eggs?

"There it is," I say to Flori. "Do you see it?"

"I can certainly smell it," she replies.

I am used to the stink of sun-dried droppings, stale grain and antiseptic, though it never fails to creep deep inside my nostrils. For Solace it must be one hundred times more intense. I can hear her searching the path with her muzzle, before pricking her ears and turning to face us.

"Are you quite sure you can control her?" Flori hangs back when she asks me this. I note the way she is looking warily at Solace.

"She won't harm you!" I scoff. "She may look fierce but you just have to trust me. Any friend of mine is a friend of Solace, too."

My torch beam is approximately half as bright as it was when I set off. So long as we don't hang around here, I feel confident that we'll make it back before the light dies entirely. For now, it's strong enough to pick out the chain-link fence that surrounds the farm and all the abandoned sheds on the other side.

The buildings are arranged like spokes on a wheel, with a giant food hopper in the centre and the night sky overhead. Floodlights reach up from the four corners, poised like giant herons, but the generator that powered them was switched off long ago. Despite the gloom, it's easy to spot the rabbits. They're out in number across the clearing surrounding the farm, grazing on nettle clumps and weeds.

"Kamil, they're *huge*! I've never seen such a well-

16

fed colony!" Without taking her eyes off her quarry, Flori slips the snare wires from her shoulder and drops to her knees to set the first trap.

"I suppose there's still a lot of chicken feed lying around," I say, noting where the rabbits have burrowed under the chain-link. "At least it isn't going to waste."

Flori moves from one burrow to another. She works so fast I can't see what she's doing with the wires, but the traps she creates look lethal.

"It's so *quiet* up here," she says at one point, and I know just what she means. Before the farm went out of business, the gabbling, scratching and clucking from this place spread so far and wide that it could be heard in our houses. Behind closed doors, throughout each day and night, a thousand hens would remind us of their existence out here, and the reasons why we were fed, clothed and housed.

From the age of fourteen up, every able-bodied man and woman found employment at the Squawk Box. With no other source of work or income to be had here, the task of raising and slaughtering poultry, then processing each unit and packing them onto the trains, was something we were practically raised to undertake. Those who worked there knew exactly how to tell when an ageing hen was about to go off the lay, which is when her days were numbered. Often she'd be slaughtered, plucked and

17

shrink-wrapped so efficiently that her final batch of eggs would be dispatched with her. Indeed, the only birds to have survived are those that managed to escape. Whenever one broke free from the Squawk Box it would always find a home in our community. Too scrawny for our tastes, such runaways were taken under wing and quietly encouraged to continue producing. Even now, those birds in our community are a little loopy, but that is no surprise when you consider what they left behind.

Now, a telling silence hangs over the place. Feathers lie scattered in the dirt still, but the birds are long gone. In this day and age, so we have been told, the demand out there is for free-range produce. People like to know that the chickens on their plates enjoyed a life foraging freely in the open air, and the Squawk Box never catered for that. Many say her owner should have foreseen such a change in demand. Still, nobody criticizes Mister Petri, who generously continues to oversee the weekly supply of provisions that began when the farm was founded by his forefathers. We may not work for such payment in kind any more, but the food parcels, though less than bountiful, are enough to keep body and soul together.

From this side of the perimeter, it is hard to get a clear view of the entire operation. If we weren't dependent on my head torch I'd take Flori all the way around to the padlocked gates for a peep at the slaughterhouse and loading platform. There, we would find ourselves standing on the single rail track. It was from here that a train would depart every day, hauling wagons away into the old brick tunnel where the woods rise. I can't say for sure where the tunnel emerges. Former workers who have ventured as far as the Grand Perimeter claim that at one time they could watch the fruit of their labours clatter out across the lowlands on the way to school kitchens and factory canteens everywhere. I should like to see the view, if only to lay eyes on the steel jaws of the animal traps said to litter each side of the track. Sadly, I just do not possess the courage. For every time I turn my attention towards the tunnel entrance, the same thing happens that persuades me not to go further: somewhere in the woods, a long distance from here, a chainsaw will begin to buzz and roar. It may well be a woodcutter at work, but the motor always cuts out just as I clear the trees for home.

Tonight, all I can hear is Solace whining softly in the darkness behind me. It's as if she too knows that time is no longer on our side.

"What will become of this place?" asks Flori, staring through the mesh.

"Never mind about that," I say, aware that what light we have left is rapidly shrinking. "Now the last chickens have been processed, what will become of *us*?"

Kamil's
Mother

Fear can take away your appetite. So too can sheer relief. I feel it every time I leave the woods behind me throughout the winter months. Each morning, having exercised Solace before sunrise, I sit for breakfast and end up feeding my dog more than I do myself.

Today, all we have left is stale crackers. Solace sits at my feet. She looks up at me like nothing else matters except what happens next, and then catches each offering in her jaws. Only when my mother drifts into the kitchen does Solace drop her head to the flagstones and pretend to be asleep, but it's too late. We've been caught.

"You mustn't forgo your food," she scolds me. "Solace can stretch out under the window all day, but you have school to attend."

As ever, my mother is dressed in her nightgown. It's as white as her hair, and hangs in thin drapes from her shoulders to her ankles. There is no meat on her any more. Ever since my father went missing, she has become a ghost of her former self.

"I can go hungry for another day," I tell her. "The supply truck will be here first thing tomorrow."

"Child, your empty belly has malnourished your mind!"

I look at her blankly. She flattens her lips, both eyes tight on me, but I am none the wiser.

"What is it?" I ask.

"The supply truck is here *today*! Unless you hurry to catch it, our cupboards will be empty for a week! Then what will I feed you? Fresh air?"

I am breathless by the time I join the queue. Only a handful of people wait patiently for their parcels, which makes me realize how late I am. I stand on the cobblestones, my hands on my knees for a moment,

She is a cool dry mad

and then look up to see if I can spot Flori. I have to lean sideways, because old Cosmina Barbescu is in front of me. Over time, Cosmina has become as formidable in size as the mountain scarp. Some say it's in her genes. Others believe she's ballooned because she only ever squeezes out of her house on delivery day. They claim she'd always been big-boned in the years when she worked at the Squawk Box. I guess the daily walk to and from the poultry farm must have kept her in shape, while holding down each chicken to clip wing after wing demanded muscle that might well have since turned to fat.

Nowadays, Cosmina Barbescu cannot move around without the aid of a walking stick or the snail-paced, four-wheeled mobility scooter my father invented for her. With an engine powered by cooking oil, and baskets mounted front and rear, it allows her to trundle around the community on days when her legs just cannot support her.

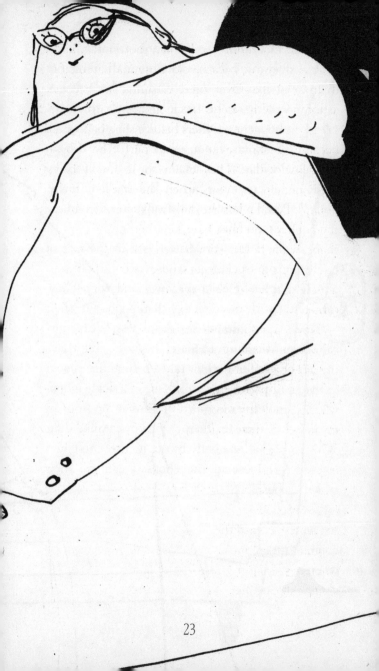

As Cosmina is on foot this morning, I can only think she has used up all the oil in her kitchen. She stands with her back to me, leaning on her stick so heavily that all I can see is an oddly small head atop sagging shoulders. From behind, I feel as if I am looking at a normal-sized lady eclipsed by an enormous pile of laundry. Eventually, I take two steps sideways in order to see around her.

I can see Mister Petri in the rear of the truck, from where he hands out supplies. He's a spry, wry and wiry fellow with more energy than anyone in their sixth decade should possess. With a jutting chin to match his nose, and what's left of his hair raked behind his ears, in profile he reminds me of a sickle moon. His two grown-up sons sit up front in the cab. They're big boys, unlike their father, both broad in the chest and loose in the chops. I can see their faces reflected in the wing mirrors, watching yet another villager hurry away with supplies for a week. It is old Wenzel, I realize. A hunched and scowling individual, so constantly bad-tempered that people wonder whether somehow he fell out with himself many years ago.

"Let me through," he grizzles, even though nobody stands in his way. In fact, he passes by so quickly that I think I must be mistaken when I spot not one parcel in his arms but *two*.

"Hey!" I wheel around as he passes, but Wenzel just keeps on moving.

"Keep an orderly line, Kamil." This is Cosmina. She speaks with a mouse-like squeak, which is strangely commanding because you expect something so much deeper. I turn to find her regarding me through horn-rimmed spectacles. Even the hoods of her eyes appear to be carrying some extra flesh. She chews on the inside of her cheeks in slow circling motions, making her chins crease and fold.

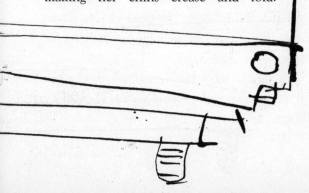

Old Wenzel

"How is your mother?" she asks. "Tell her to eat. She has to eat if she wants to get strong again. Unless she eats, she won't survive."

"I'll tell her," I say, though I'm still distracted by what the last villager has just taken. I watch him go and wonder if perhaps he's picked up an extra package for a neighbour. When I face back to Cosmina, I find her regarding me like she's just read my mind.

"We only want what's best," she tells me, and promptly fills the space at the head of the queue. "While the lean times last, we have to watch out for each other."

I choose not to reply, because somebody else has her full attention now, and he is the reason why we are all here.

"Cosmina! Almost last but never least." Mister Petri is standing at the edge of his truck with his shirtsleeves rolled up and both hands on his waistband. The sun may have yet to warm the day, but it's clear he has worked up a sweat. He wipes his brow, and then beams fondly at the big lady in front of me. "How delightful to see you looking so well!"

"Oh, stop it! I'm blushing!" In her tent-sized dress, with a hemline touching the ground, Cosmina Barbescu glides forward as if moving on tentacles. From a shelf inside his truck, Mister Petri selects a parcel and loads it into the hook of her arm.

"Is there liver pâté?" she asks. "I just *adore* your liver pâté."

Mister Petri seems both amused and surprised. "Most people ask me to leave the liver pâté *out*, Cosmina."

"It isn't for everyone," she agrees.

I swap a glance with Mister Petri. The look on his face makes me think he wouldn't touch the stuff personally, and I understand why. Even Solace found the greasy meat and jelly hard to swallow, but we did so because we had no other choice.

"Let me see if I have any to spare." With a sigh, he disappears to the shelves at the back of his truck.

Watching him go, I decide that if Cosmina could stomach an extra tin of such muck a week then nobody would object.

27

"You're very kind," she says, when Mister Petri returns with her prize. He wedges a can between the parcel and her chins, and then watches as she turns on her stick to leave. When he finally focuses on me, he does so with a grin I quickly share.

"At least the waddle back will do her some good," he says. "Now tell me, Kamil, has your mother's appetite returned? I know she has a long way to go before she can match Cosmina, but if she wastes away any further I fear we may lose her altogether."

"She misses my father more than a good meal," I say. "But she takes good care of me."

"You're a fortunate boy," replies Mister Petri, and hands down my food parcel. "I'm only sorry that I can't provide any more."

MISTER PETRI

"We are very grateful," I say. "Though with luck we may have rabbit for our stewpots this week."

"I admire your instinct for survival, young man." Mister Petri crouches now so his gaze meets mine directly. Underneath those white bushy brows, his eyes are really quite youthful. "I hear the meadow can be easy pickings."

"It's better in the woods," I say, and then remind myself who I am speaking to here. When I look up it's clear that Mister Petri knows just where I mean.

"There are plenty of burrows around the Squawk Box, Kamil, but the rabbits that dwell in them are not healthy. Eating them would be unwise."

"But they're so plump!" I say in surprise.

"Fit to burst, in fact." Mister Petri beckons me closer. "Whatever illness has afflicted those poor bunnies causes their stomachs to swell with gas until eventually they … how can I put this? They literally *explode*!" He curls a finger into the corner of his mouth. When he pulls it out, the popping sound makes me blink and shrink back a step. "My sons and I find them in the enclosure from time to time. It isn't pleasant. A mess like that can take several shovels to clear, and I'd hate to dispatch them to clear up anything larger."

5

I can see the meadow from my desk in the schoolhouse. Sitting next to the window, I often find my attention drawn to the distant fringe of trees. If I focus for a long time, especially on a breezy day, the sway of the branches can begin to look like the woods are breathing in and out.

This afternoon, all is very still. The mist remains with us. Having rolled down the mountain for the morning, it has now seeped into the woods. There's not a breath of wind, and yet somehow I detect movement over there. I think that if I keep on look-ing then something will reveal itself to me. I am ready for anything, but for the voice that drags me back to my desk.

"*Are you with us, Kamil? Are you listening?*"

I blink, gasp, and hurriedly face the figure in front of the blackboard. She's smartly dressed, with straw-blonde hair tied up in a bun and little round glasses framing her freckled face.

Miss Milea

"Yes, Miss Milea."

"Then what is the answer?"

I open my mouth, even though I'm lost for words, and feel relief when a cowbell begins to peal from the courtyard. At first, Miss Milea ignores the signal for the end of the day's class. She holds my gaze, awaiting my response as a brace of pupils rush for the door.

"Can I tell you tomorrow?" I ask, and she laughs despite herself.

I like Miss Milea. She showed me great kindness when my father went missing. Everyone enjoys her lessons. All the girls in my class think she is as pretty as a posy, which makes it so sad that two fingers from her left hand are missing at the knuckle. Nobody likes to ask her how this happened, but as

31

Miss Milea spent the first few years of her working life at the Squawk Box, it isn't hard to guess what occurred. If it's true, despite the sadness left by the poultry farm's closure, I think she must be much happier handling children than heavy machinery. Right now, clasping her bad hand inside her good hand as usual, Miss Milea makes me wait a moment for an answer. Then her stern expression softens into something far more natural.

"Mark my words, Kamil, I will ask you again when lessons start tomorrow. And if you need to know the question," she finishes, turning to the one pupil waiting for me, "I'm sure Flori will refresh your memory."

The first thing my friend asks, before we've even left the classroom, is the last thing I want to consider.

"What time shall we leave for the Squawk Box? I cannot wait to check the traps."

I walk on, shaking my head. "That isn't a good idea, Flori."

"Why not? Solace needs her exercise. You're always telling me that."

"Not this evening. I'll play with her in the meadow until sundown."

As soon as I say this, Flori looks astonished.

"You can't *play* with a dog like Solace. Kamil, she needs her walk in the woods."

All of a sudden I am aware that Miss Milea is still

watching us. I want to leave the classroom. I'd like to be clear of the schoolhouse altogether so I can speak freely, but Flori just will not let it go.

"I dreamed about those rabbits," she tells me. "If I snared one that size my father would be lost for words! I'll go on my own if I must, but I'd sooner walk there with you."

Flori holds my gaze, and for a moment I think she might grasp my wrists too. Miss Milea is wiping the blackboard down with her good hand, but I am sure she is tuned into every word.

"Forget about the Squawk Box," I tell her eventually. "Just forget it."

Confusion clouds my friend's expression, but then her attention switches across the classroom. I turn and find Miss Milea preparing to leave.

"You should listen to Kamil," she says, approaching the door with a pile of school books in her arms. "The poultry farm is no place for children."

Our teacher says no more. She just leaves us with a cautionary glance.

Flori faces back to me looking more inquisitive than ever.

"Miss Milea is not the first person today to warn me to stay away," I say under my breath. "When I collected my parcel this morning, Mister Petri advised me to steer clear of the burrows up there."

"But why?"

"He asked me not to breathe a word, for fear of spreading panic. If I tell you, Flori, you must swear to keep it a secret."

"You can trust me, Kamil. A poacher knows when to keep quiet."

With a glance over my shoulder, I tell her that the rabbits are unwell. I explain that the illness causes their insides to swell until they burst. I even finish by making the same popping sound as Mister Petri.

A moment passes. Flori looks shocked. Then she laughs long and hard.

"Kamil, those rabbits are big because they eat well!"

"But Mister Petri is concerned that the disease might pass on to us if we come into contact with a sick bunny."

"Mister Petri is having fun at your expense," she grins. "I've never heard such nonsense!"

"I just think it best that we stay away from the Squawk Box," I say, feeling foolish all the same.

"On the contrary," replies Flori with glee. "We should prepare to check the snares."

"No way!" I shake my head. "I'm not setting foot in the woods tonight."

"What's stopping you?" she asks, as one side of her mouth arches into a playful grin. "Are you *scared?*"

Thirty minutes. That's all we have before the head torch leaves us at the mercy of the night. I remind Flori of this once at my garden gate, again as we follow Solace across the meadow, and finally when we clasp the mesh and peer into the poultry farm.

"Except now we only have half that time left," I add. "We really shouldn't be here for long."

Tonight, with the moon behind clouds, the sky could be made from marble. Mist hangs in veils over the enclosure, which eddies in places where invisible currents are at work. The roosting sheds stand dark and forbidding within it, like rocks in a treacherous sea. Flori is wearing her woollen cap once more, and has turned up the collar of her camouflage coat. Like Solace, panting at our feet, her every breath turns to vapour in the air. She doesn't look at me when I repeat how important it is for us to turn back soon. She just smiles to herself, clearly relishing my uneasiness.

"Trust me," she whispers, and begins to inspect her snares. "Tomorrow you'll watch your mother stirring the stewpot and wonder what it was you had to fear."

"I'm not hungry," I say. "I'm really not hungry at all."

I remember feeling uncomfortable the very first time my father brought me to the Squawk Box. I had seen plenty of chickens, of course. Every other yard in our community contained the odd rescue hen, but nothing could have prepared me for that scene. It was the sheer scale of the operation that troubled me back then. I will never forget emerging from behind my father to face a seething mass of poultry, and being struck by the sense that every single hen was aware of my presence. Wherever I looked, thousands of sharp little eyes would follow me. My father found it amusing, but didn't protest when I asked if he could take me home. I dwell on this as I look around now. For there isn't a single chicken in sight, and yet all I want to do is back away.

Then I realize it isn't the absence of the poultry that has left me so on edge. Unlike last night, there are no rabbits to be seen grazing within the enclosure. I am about to point this out to Flori, but find her returning with something to tell me first.

"Nothing," she says, sounding as surprised as she does disappointed. "Not even a sniff. Every single snare has been left untouched. All I found was this," she adds, and uncurls her hand to show me. "It's supposed to bring good luck, so I feel somewhat cheated."

"Flori, you shouldn't be touching things like that." In her palm is a rabbit's paw. I do not like the look of it one bit. "What if it's from a bunny that's exploded?"

Flori scoffs at the suggestion, and waves it in front of me. "It's probably been chewed off, Kamil!"

"By what?"

"A predator of some sort." She shrugs and kicks at the dirt. "Maybe whatever claimed the rest of this one for its supper has scared off the others. All the rabbits in this colony have gone to ground."

"So can we please leave now? We really don't have much time left."

"Very well," she says, and pockets the rabbit's foot. "Perhaps it'll bring me good fortune next time we check the snares. A good poacher must be patient, that much I know."

Flori breaks away from the mesh. It rattles and sings as she does so, but I don't feel as jumpy now I know we're on our way back. Solace leads the way, trotting under the vaulted tunnel of branches so swiftly that for a moment she leaves the reach of my torch beam. When I catch up with her again, I find her standing square across the path, ears pricked and facing me.

"What is it?" asks Flori, and that's when Solace growls. A low, measured warning that brings me to a sudden halt. Immediately, I feel a sense of dread crawl over me, for her attention is fixed on a point behind us. I turn with my friend, only to gasp and shrink behind the nearest tree trunk.

"Take off your head torch!" Flori urges under her breath. She sounds startled, and for very good reason.

I grab Solace by the collar and touch my finger to my lips. Then I brace myself to steal another look at the poultry farm. The trunk we're behind is broad and twisted, as if it too is straining to see what's going on back there. With my breath bated, I peer out from behind it. Through the mist, under the mottled moonlight, I simply stare at the cause of our alarm.

At the front of the enclosure, inside the slaughterhouse where the chickens once met their fate, a lantern is burning brightly.

It is hanging from a meat hook over a steel-topped table, both of which are framed by a porthole window. Judging by the shadow thrown across the

interior wall, I know that someone with a butcher's build is in there even before he steps into view. Facing away from the glass, this bulky, bald-headed figure hauls on a pair of industrial gloves and then hoists a pail onto the table.

"Who is it?" asks Flori. "Who's in there?"

"I can't say for sure," I tell her. "But he's scrubbing down the surfaces."

I face Flori. My head torch is lying at her feet. What little light is left shines directly upwards. It's enough to capture the startled look on her face. She doesn't blink. She doesn't even appear to breathe.

Now I know for sure what has caused the rabbits

to steer clear. I just wish we had done the same thing.

In the stillness, we hear the sound of slopping water and bristles scratching over steel. Maybe that's all it takes to push Solace's instinct to protect us, because all of a sudden she's barking and snarling and straining against my grasp with such force that she slips away completely.

"Get the dog under control!" cries Flori, aghast as Solace sprints for the perimeter. "She'll give us away!"

"It's too late," I tell her, aware that the man in the window has turned around. At the same time, a second source of light sways into view from behind the central feed hopper. It seems to hover like a firefly, and then rise by several feet. That's when I see another figure just behind it, and realize he's holding a lantern aloft. He shouts something at Solace, but the dog is making such an almighty racket that it's impossible to understand. He advances towards the chain-link fence by several steps, and then breaks for a gate I had always believed to be locked.

"We can't stay here," cries Flori, tugging at my sleeve, and I agree with her. I just refuse to abandon my dog. For the bald-domed brute from the slaughterhouse is also out in the open air now. Only he's brandishing a chop knife instead of a lantern. I see the dog tear round the meshing to confront him at the gate. I know she'll fight to the death for me, and fear the worst might happen.

"Solace!" I yell, stepping out into the path. "*Run, Solace!*"

I leave these last words to hang in the air as I turn and flee. Flori has already taken off into the darkness. I can hear her footfalls on the path some way ahead. My heart is kicking at the same rate inside my chest, and not just because I'm sprinting as fast I can.

I sense a presence close behind, rapidly gathering ground, and a cry dies in my throat before I realize it is Solace. She shoots past, a pale white wraith in the night, and I know that I cannot lose sight of her. For in the chaos I have left the head torch behind. We are running nearly blind now, but I know this dense section of woods well enough to work out where I am. Every turn and dip is familiar, and when Flori stumbles on an exposed root I am there to grab her by the elbow. I can even tell when we are close to the edge of the woods, and the meadow that will take us safely home. Sure enough, through the gloom I begin to make out the shapes of trees at the fringes and dotted lights from the cottages and shacks beyond. I laugh in sheer relief, and turn to share it with Flori. At the same time, she slows so abruptly I think she might backtrack.

"We're nearly through, Flori! Don't stop yet!"

"We can't go on!"

"Why not?" I say breathlessly, aware now that she's focused on something at the mouth of the path. Solace runs back to us just then, and for one awful moment I think the fellows we had disturbed in the Squawk Box might have found a short cut. Then I see what my friend has spotted, there in a shaft of moonlight,

and my jaw falls.

"What is it?"

We approach with great caution. As we come close it feels unnaturally cold. I even note the faintest ring of frost around the object of our attention. What we're looking at is clearly lifeless, but I still crouch before it with some caution. For we're faced with a monstrous creation. A raven, I think, with its beak buried deep into the ground and one broken wing fanned wide.

It looks as if it's been thrown like a spear, such is the angle of this stiffened corpse and the scattering of black feathers, but somehow I feel sure it has been placed here with great care.

"What are those *things?*" asks Flori in a small voice, and I know just what she's looking at. I recognize the bony beaks and the saucer-like eye sockets.

"Chicken skulls," I say, aghast, for that's what they are. Four in total, one stacked on top of the other, and bound to the back of this bird as if hitching a ride to hell. "But is it meant for us?"

Flori looks across at me. "All I know," she says fearfully, "is that it wasn't here when we entered the woods."

As she speaks, I hear twigs snapping some distance behind us. I turn to see two lantern lights through the trees, and grasp Solace by her collar once again.

"Let's not worry about that now." I help Flori to her feet. "We can always take another look at it in daylight."

"Kamil, I'm never coming back again!" She steps around our gruesome discovery and begins the last leg for home. "Something very bad is happening in these woods. Something *frightening*. I'm not too proud to admit it, but I'm scared. And if you know what's good for you, Kamil, you should be scared, too!"

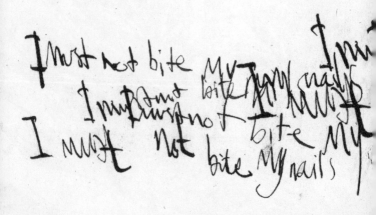

not
is not bite bite my
not bite my nails my nai
li

7

No church has ever existed in
this community. Instead, at its heart is
a green open space. A stream divides it that
swells when the rain runs off the mountain. The
stream snakes around a great beech tree. The leaves
dropped months ago. In these lean times, I wonder
if they'll ever grow again.

For the past few days, since Flori and I fled from
the woods in terror, I have brought Solace here. I
throw her sticks to stretch her legs. On the cusp of
daylight and when night falls, this is where I exercise
my dog. I have to be careful where I toss each stick,
of course. When the poultry farm closed, several
resourceful souls fenced off a section of the green for

planting vegetables. It seemed like a wise plan at the time. Mister Petri and his sons may have pledged to continue funding our basic supplies, but everything came in cartons, jars and tins. If we needed fresh produce, we would have to grow our own.

Unfortunately, none of us have experience in raising crops. Processing hens might be in our blood, as I am reminded by the sound of all the rescued specimens across the community rising for the day, but germinating seeds and encouraging shoots to thrive just isn't in our nature. Right now, meagre pumpkins stud the soil. Most of these pale orange globes are peppered with maggot holes. This won't stop the harvest being turned into a thin and tasteless soup – one that often comes with unwelcome chewy bits – but it's the best that we can do. As nobody would thank me if I let Solace trample all over the produce, I fling the stick in the opposite direction. It doesn't give her far to run, and though it means that we are watched, at least I know by whom.

"That's no way to exercise a dog, Kamil. A dog needs a good long walk. A walk in the woods is what she needs. She'll grow fat without a walk. Fat and aggressive. Mark my words, a dog without exercise will turn on you one day. Then you'll be sorry."

Cosmina Barbescu addresses me through the kitchen window of her cottage. The walls are painted white and host to creeping roses. I note her mobility scooter parked beside the door, with all four wheels tipped slightly inwards, and wonder briefly whether my father had designed it to carry a load that just grew heavier and heavier. It is not quite dawn, but her oil lamps were blazing when I arrived. I can see a pot boiling on the stove behind her, and wonder what she's slow-cooking this early in the day. When Cosmina leans out over the ledge, she practically fills the frame.

"Solace would never turn on me," I call back. "She knows I am trying my best."

Cosmina holds a tin in one hand and a spoon in the other. At first I think she is going to offer something to Solace. Instead, she scrapes out what is left for herself. As she does so, I hear a sudden rise in the level of clucking from the yard next door. Cosmina slides her attention to the shack that occupies the plot beside her cottage. It's in a tumbledown state, hammered together from tarred planks and topped off by mismatched tiles thick with moss.

"Hey, Wenzel?" she calls over the fence between them, frowning irritably. "Wake up, old man! Your hens are becoming unruly!"

Though the curtains are drawn and the windows closed, we both hear the old man shouting at Cosmina to mind her own business. She looks at me, as if to be sure she has heard him correctly, and pinks at the cheeks.

"I'm sure they'll calm down," I say, anxious not to be caught up in any kind of conflict between neighbours.

"Every time I eat," she says, glaring once again at Wenzel's property. "They go crazy when I eat."

"It must be a coincidence," is all I can offer.

I would suggest to Cosmina that it must be hard for her to know what's normal for Wenzel's flock, since she spends most of her time with her mouth full. I just don't wish to appear rude. So I keep it to myself, even though the hens do sound unusually disturbed, and make a fuss of Solace instead.

"Take her to the woods," she advises me. "What is wrong with the woods?"

"I've lost my head torch," I say.

"Careless, careless boy!"

I want to tell her about the old poultry farm. I draw breath to confess that I have seen activity up there, but say nothing. In the light of each day that has passed since then, I don't think anyone would believe me. What really persuades me to stay quiet is the thought of the feather and bone creation that stopped us in our tracks. Cosmina would only pull a face at me, like she'd just chewed something sour, and insist that I had dreamed it.

"It's just too dark in the woods without my torch," I tell her, raising my voice to be heard. "And I can't wait until sunrise as it means I'll be late for school."

Cosmina returns her spoon to the tin, regarding me through those horn-rimmed spectacles of hers. "What would your father say?" she asks eventually. "Your father was never scared of the dark."

"He wasn't scared of *anything*!" I reply, so abruptly that the chickens actually fall quiet. Embarrassed now, I look to my shoes. "But maybe I'm not so courageous."

In the silence, I hear Cosmina breathe out through her nostrils.

"Your father was very proud of you, Kamil. Very proud indeed."

I look up at this, just as she closes the kitchen window. Several hens start to cluck once more, but nothing like the din they had just kicked up. Cosmina Barbescu regards me through the glass, misted up on the inside from all that cooking, and then waddles back to her stove. Solace returns to my side. She has the stick clamped in her jaws. When I meet her eyes, she drops it at my feet. I pick it up and throw it for her. My dog doesn't move. She just

51

looks at me pleadingly, and I know that tonight I will have to face my fears. For Solace's sake as much as my own, I must return to the woods.

AB<sub>c</sub> Defghij-
= BAD

"Kamil, you're as crazy as the chickens! Only a fool would dare to go back."

Flori speaks her mind in a whisper, and with a handkerchief balled in one hand. She's sitting beside me in the schoolhouse classroom. Miss Milea is facing the blackboard. She's writing out sums to test us all. As Flori had been complaining about a sore throat and a head cold all morning, I did not expect her to flare up like this.

"I won't go near the poultry farm," I say under my breath, watching Miss Milea for a sign that she has heard. "If I stay on the path I am sure no harm will come to me. Even without my head torch, I believe I can find my way home again."

53

"Are you forgetting the warning?" she counters. "That raven creation was meant for us, Kamil. Somebody is trying to keep us out of the woods."

"How can we be sure it's a warning?" I ask. "Maybe it's a good luck charm!"

Flori glares at me witheringly. "A good luck charm? A dead bird with four skulls strapped to its back? And how do you explain the drop in temperature? It left me cold for many different reasons, Kamil."

"The frost probably crept in from the meadow," I say. "It's open to the night sky out there, and can get very chilly."

"There can be no innocent explanation for what we saw," she says, fretting at her handkerchief now. "Whatever it means, if you had any sense you'd stay out of the woods and keep *quiet*!"

At this, Miss Milea turns to face Flori directly. "Quiet is all I ask for in this classroom," she says. "If there's something you'd like to share with Kamil, perhaps you could tell us all."

I feel my cheeks heat as she speaks, and summon the courage to defend my friend.

"I'm sorry," I say. "I just asked Flori a question."

"A question about algebra, I trust."

"Of course."

I know Miss Milea doesn't believe me, but then Flori sneezes and blows her nose. Immediately, her concern switches to my friend.

"Your eyes seem puffy, Flori. Are you feeling unwell?"

"I will be fine," she says, only to sneeze once more. "It's just a winter cold."

Miss Milea places her chalk on the desk, and crosses the floor to her side. All eyes turn to face Flori. Miss Milea feels her forehead, and immediately orders her home.

"You have a fever," she says, and looks across at me. "Kamil will make sure that you get back safely."

Flori faces round to me, sniffling still, and holds my gaze for a moment. "I can manage on my own," she says finally, and rises with her school books. As Miss Milea returns to the front of the classroom, Flori catches my eye one more time. "It is *you* who should be concerned about getting home safe and sound."

I watch her leave, wishing I had said nothing, and try to concentrate on my schoolwork. Miss Milea knows how to test us. Some of the multiplications and divisions on the blackboard make my head spin, but then I know that I am distracted. Instead of writing out numbers, within minutes I find myself sketching the raven. As I draw the bird I recall details about it that had slipped my mind, like the way its wings flopped over and the loose feathers on the ground. I add each chicken skull, hoping

55

perhaps it will make more sense to me than the sums. It looks like nothing on earth, however, no matter which way I turn it.

"Kamil, are you feeling poorly too?"

At once I fold my arms over the page, and find Miss Milea at the limit of her patience with me. She is not the kind of teacher who would ever lose her temper, but when she speaks this calmly it is clear that she is cross. I say nothing, aware that I have been caught, and dutifully turn the sheet of paper so I can start again.

This time, aware that I am being watched, the solution to the first sum comes quickly to me. I glance up at Miss Milea, who smiles. I contemplate the next sum, start to work it out on the page, and then stop with such a jolt that I break the tip of the pencil. I flip the page, look at the sketch once again, and realize that neither the raven nor the chickens are of concern right now.

*It is the rabbits.*

Mister Petri himself warned me to steer clear of the poultry farm. He said that something was not right with the warren up there. Flori was the first to dismiss such a claim. She was the one who insisted that I take her so she could lay some traps. When my friend picked up that bunny's paw it didn't feel like a good luck charm to me. Quite the opposite, in fact.

And now Flori has been taken ill with a fever.

"Miss Milea?" I raise my hand. Judging by the way she arches one eyebrow, I believe she knows what I am going to say before I even draw breath to tell her. "I am not feeling so well myself all of a sudden. May I be excused?"

I find Flori's father in his backyard, scattering seeds for his chickens. Having knocked twice on the cottage door, I just followed the sound of contented clucking.

"Do you know what I like best of all about hens?" he asks, by way of greeting.

"What would that be?"

"I like that they're so *giving*. All they require is a little sustenance, some tender loving care and a warm place to roost at night. In return, you'll never go short of eggs."

Flori's father is weather-beaten in appearance, but so sturdy I doubt that anything could ever knock him over. Half a dozen ginger and black chickens surround his feet, pecking at the treats as dusk closes in. They're scrawny specimens, reared as they were on the poultry farm, with missing feathers and little meat on their bones. Despite their sorry appearance, these birds have learned how to please their newfound owners and avoid the fate for which they were bred. Some say that even the chickens know it would be curtains if they ever stopped laying on a daily basis.

"They're very fortunate to have a keeper like you."

Even as I say this, I know that Flori's father would have no hesitation in dispatching any bird that failed to provide for him. They would go the same way as the brace of wild pigeons I can see hanging from a hook inside his shed. I would never question a man like this about his profession. I have even heard it said that the poacher before me often dares to ignore the roar of the chainsaw and has set traps as far as the Grand Perimeter. Judging by his stalking coat, broad-brimmed hat, and the fact that the sun has sunk behind the great scarp, I think he must be preparing to go to work soon. He would never admit to such a thing, of course. Then again, I am the one who is here to make a confession.

"How is Flori?" I ask, steeling myself to tell him what I know.

One of the hens picks up on my presence just then. She looks at me with her head cocked, and then backs away squabbling with herself.

"Flori has taken to her bed," he replies, observing the bird. "It is nothing that a good sleep and a mug of hot elder tea can't cure."

"I'm not so sure it's a winter cold."

At once, before he can respond, the chicken fans her wings and squawks. I swap a glance with Flori's father, and watch as she sprints haphazardly to the far end of the yard.

"Something's spooked her," he tells me as she turns around to return the way she came. This time, flapping furiously as she passes, the bird lifts away from the ground for a moment. "Often these old girls pick up on threats before us," he says, squinting as he peers into the evening sky. "They're primed to be on the lookout at all times."

As he tells me this, I think of all the fuss and clucking I'd heard while talking to Cosmina. "Maybe a fox has crept into the community," I suggest.

Flori's father dismisses the suggestion with a chuckle. "A fox would help himself to the rabbits in my traps before moving on to the chickens, and I've seen no evidence of that."

I swallow uncomfortably. "What if the rabbits were sick? Would a fox avoid them if they're unwell?"

"That depends on how desperate and hungry he is. A fox will eat *anything* if his survival depends on it."

61

Where is old foxy, eh?

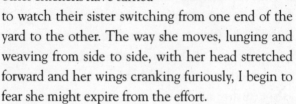

By now, even the other chickens have turned to watch their sister switching from one end of the yard to the other. The way she moves, lunging and weaving from side to side, with her head stretched forward and her wings cranking furiously, I begin to fear she might expire from the effort.

"Sir," I say, and take a deep breath. "I think Flori has the same sickness as the rabbits around the Squawk Box."

"What sickness?" he asks, turning to me now. "Speak up, Kamil."

"Mister Petri warned me it could be most unpleasant. Something that makes their insides swell until they burst!" I look to the ground between us. "Flori walked Solace through the woods with me recently. We went all the way to the clearing around the poultry farm. She saw the size of the rabbits there and laid traps. She even picked up a paw for good luck. Now I'm scared she might be next to pop!"

Only the restless hen prevents silence from falling upon us. Each time she hurtles across the yard, she tries to take flight. At every attempt, her feet just reconnect with the ground.

"Kamil," he says finally, and I lift my gaze to

find him looking most amused. He gestures at the chicken as she makes another run. "You're as cooked in the head as she is. The only difference is that the hens in this community have reason to be a little unbalanced. Any bird that escapes from a poultry farm is bound to be disturbed by the experience of their time inside. If there's a predator around then I would know about it, too. I can't smell a fox and nor is there a hawk overhead, which means it's all in her imagination. Just as this sickness with the rabbits is all in yours. Rabbits can die of many causes, but I have never seen one explode. Flori simply needs to rest. Much like my poor hen!"

I take in what the poacher has said, and wish his daughter well. As soon as I turn to leave, he calls me back.

"What is it?" I ask.

"I have something that might make life easier for you." He strides across to his shed, pausing only for the chicken as she sprints across his path. Inside, having steered around the dangling brace of pigeons, he returns with an object from his work-bench that I never thought I would see again.

"The strap is a little damp from the overnight dew," he tells me, "but I have no doubt it'll work just fine."

"My head torch! How did you find it?" I meet his eyes, as pale and blue as his daughter's.

"I know the woods," he says eventually. "There are many spots where I can be sure my snares won't be empty for long, but the clearing around the Squawk Box is one I have chosen not to test. That Mister Petri has been moved to spin a story about exploding rabbits just reminds me why I go no further than the sidelines, which is where I found your torch. The man is as private as he is generous with our provisions, Kamil, and I do not wish to earn his displeasure by straying too close to the poultry farm."

I turn the head torch in my hands, and take this as a warning to stay away myself.

"Can I ask you something, sir? Something else about the woods."

"Of course."

"Did you come across a dead raven on the path? A raven with four chicken skulls bound to its back."

Flori's father looks bemused. "I saw no such thing, Kamil. All I can tell you is that the raven is a symbol of darkness and death. As for chicken skulls, I know of no such folklore. It just sounds like the stuff of nightmares."

I look him in the eye. He does not drop my gaze.

"It was," I agree. "And I cannot forget it."

27 - 10 + 1 - 12
27 - 10 + 1 - 12
27 - 10 + 1 - 12

**1**

Everyone knows that my father was a gifted inventor, as Cosmina's mobility scooter demonstrated. They still remember him for his tiny teardrop troughs, designed to assist those who wished to record how much they cried in their sleep. The reverse telescope was met with little enthusiasm, for nobody believed that entire galaxies could be seen within the orb of a human eye, and yet his attempts to improve our lives were always much admired.

My father didn't demonstrate the pedal-powered head torch to anyone but his family. This was because he created it only to walk Solace after dark. I should be relieved that it is back in my possession, but that is not how I feel.

I have been in the meadow for no more than a minute, wrapped up against the chill and with my fingers tightly crossed. I'm not scared. I am simply *terrified*.

The moon is beginning to fill. A few nights from now it will hang like a mothball over the woods. Tonight, it casts enough light to throw shadows. As I approach the towering tree line, with Solace just ahead, several rabbits scatter from our path. They look perfectly healthy, as I keep reminding myself, just as they would be around the Squawk Box.

"It's all in my mind," I tell myself. "Remember what the poacher said."

Ahead, moonshine breaks through the tree canopy in beams. I hold my head up high, but not because I am feeling courageous. I am just anxious to find the mouth of the path with my torch. When I do so, with bated breath, I find the dead raven has disappeared. I am not surprised, however. There are many hungry mouths in the woods as well as in the community. Rather than push on, I call Solace back. She appears in the pool of light, looking a little confused, but this is how I have planned her walk tonight.

"Come along," I say, trying to make this sound fun for her. "I'll race you back across the meadow."

I had hatched the idea from watching the crazy chicken. Seeing her pelt from one end of the yard to the other made me realize that my dog might benefit from something similar. In half an hour, I could cross the meadow a dozen times. I don't want to be out here one little bit, of course, but Solace's needs come first.

With my back to the woods this walk feels much easier. Indeed, when I turn to face the tree line again it does not seem like such a test of nerves. When a bat shrieks I barely flinch. I even pause to watch it twist and swoop over the meadow right in front of us. Solace trots onwards. She knows there are times when a chase would be futile.

So, when her ears stiffen and she bolts for the woods, I know she has locked on to something she just can't ignore.

"Come back!" I call after her, and break into a run. "Don't do this to me!"

I reach the mouth of the path. There is no sign of her, so I stop to listen. The beam from my head torch sweeps between the trees. I realize I am standing just where the dead raven was. I take a step backwards. There is no way I want to step further into these woods right now.

"Where are you?" I call, but without much force in it. All of a sudden I really don't want to make my presence known. I feel very small indeed.

*Quiet, dog!*

"Solace, *please!*"

I strain to listen for some kind of response. Despite the stillness of the night, I hear nothing. Not even a twig dropping. It is as if the woods have just taken a deep breath. I retreat by another step, unnerved by the silence, and then take to my heels when that is shattered by a scream.

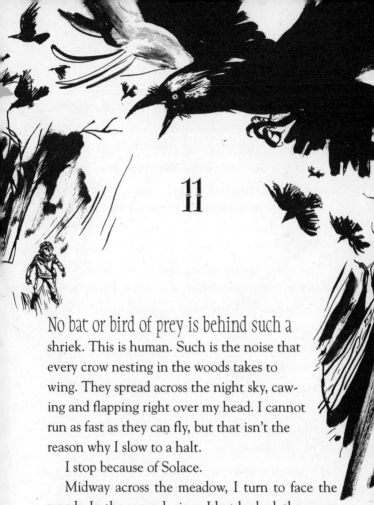

# 11

No bat or bird of prey is behind such a shriek. This is human. Such is the noise that every crow nesting in the woods takes to wing. They spread across the night sky, cawing and flapping right over my head. I cannot run as fast as they can fly, but that isn't the reason why I slow to a halt.

I stop because of Solace.

Midway across the meadow, I turn to face the woods. In the seconds since I last looked, the upper branches seem to have spread in height. They even appear to be swaying under the stars. My heart is kicking like a mule, but unless I am to ignore my responsibilities I know that I must follow the path.

As I retrace my steps, I am drawn to thinking about what happened to my father. Back then, he went into the woods but only Solace came out. I cannot bear to tell my mother that our family's beloved dog has been lost as well.

"Solace?" I call out eventually. I am in the depths now, where the path winds so much it is hard to work out which direction I'm facing. *"Solace!"*

I know that my voice will betray my presence. I just hope that my dog finds me first.

*"Kamil?"*

The voice breaks out of the gloom. Whoever is behind it is off the path, but so close I nearly trip over myself to stop and train my head torch into the undergrowth.

"Who is it?"

"Over here!"

I think I recognize the voice this time. I just can't believe I might be right. With great care I ease a passage through the tangled, thorny thicket. Beyond, in a small clearing dotted with toadstools, I find my dog beside a crouching figure.

"Miss Milea!" My torch shines into her face as I drop down beside her. Solace nuzzles me and whines. "What are you doing here?"

My teacher is wearing a thick coat, a woolly hat with green earmuffs and a matching pair of mittens. She looks very awkward indeed.

70

"I overheard you speaking to Flori in class," she says in the same hushed tone as me.

"About the Squawk Box?"

"I used to work there, Kamil. Conditions were terrible, and not just for the chickens." I note her curl her bad hand as she says this. It may be clad in a mitten, but it must be something she can never forget. "When the farm closed down I believe I was alone in being thankful. We may live in lean times now but everyone is safe from harm. If I thought for a moment that the poultry farm was preparing to go back into business I would be the first to protest. So, I had to come here and find out for myself."

"Weren't you scared?" I ask. "You don't even have a torch."

"I'm so scared I'm *shaking*!" she replies, but musters a smile for me. "When Solace bounded up to me, I jumped out of my skin. All I could hear was the sound of a panting beast hurtling along the path behind me. Is it any wonder that I screamed?"

We both turn our attention to the dog. She turns away from us, as if keeping watch.

"There's no need to be scared of Solace," I assure

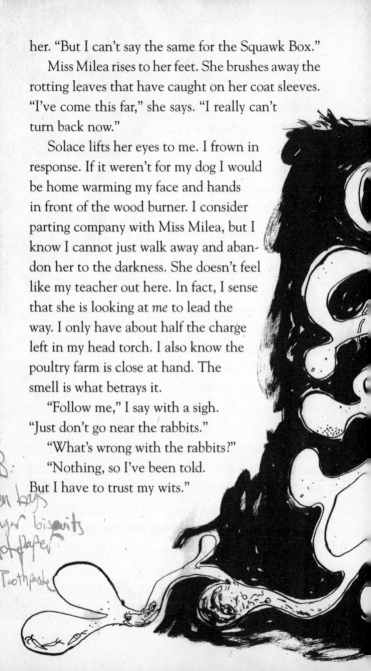

her. "But I can't say the same for the Squawk Box."

Miss Milea rises to her feet. She brushes away the rotting leaves that have caught on her coat sleeves. "I've come this far," she says. "I really can't turn back now."

Solace lifts her eyes to me. I frown in response. If it weren't for my dog I would be home warming my face and hands in front of the wood burner. I consider parting company with Miss Milea, but I know I cannot just walk away and abandon her to the darkness. She doesn't feel like my teacher out here. In fact, I sense that she is looking at *me* to lead the way. I only have about half the charge left in my head torch. I also know the poultry farm is close at hand. The smell is what betrays it.

"Follow me," I say with a sigh. "Just don't go near the rabbits."

"What's wrong with the rabbits?"

"Nothing, so I've been told. But I have to trust my wits."

12

It feels odd to be in charge. Miss Milea follows close behind. It's so dark that she even places a mittened hand on my shoulder as I guide her round a boggy stretch of the path.

"Are *you* scared?" she asks.

I tell her what my father used to say, if only to avoid answering her truthfully. For as the Squawk Box looms into view, fenced off in that clearing surrounded by warrens, it is plain some kind of activity is taking place. This time, lamps are burning not just inside the slaughterhouse but also in some of the nearby build-ings. I hear the slow, rhythmical scraping sound of steel upon steel coming from one of them, which is more than enough for me. With one hand clutching Solace's collar, I turn to Miss Milea and find her face in my fading torchlight.

"This is as far as we should go," I warn. "Mister Petri would not take kindly to finding us at this hour. He has already advised me not to come here."

I make room for her behind the twisted oak tree. A glance at the burrows surrounding the poultry farm reveals several rabbits grazing under the stars out there. They're really just dark shapes, which makes it impossible for me to see if any are fit to blow apart.

"But what does he have to hide?" she asks. "And why can we not hear any chickens?"

I had not considered this last time, and nor had Flori. If the Squawk Box was beginning to process poultry once again, surely the roosting sheds would be the focus of attention here. They'd need scrub-bing and disinfecting long before the slaughterhouse was required. Of greater concern to me is the fact that we do not have much light left. There is no way now that my head torch will see us safely out of the woods. I just have this feeling we should get as far as we can before it fades away completely.

"Perhaps Mister Petri will make an announcement

soon," I suggest, but already I know that I have lost her. "Please, Miss Milea, we must go back!"

"Just let me take a closer look first," she says. "I have to see what's going on."

All I can do is restrain Solace and watch helplessly as my teacher creeps towards the chain-link fence. At once the rabbits scatter. Several struggle to move as swiftly. A few just lope out of her line of sight and continue to graze. I see no sign of anyone outside the buildings, which is a small relief, but with every step she takes my heart quickens. Solace begins to whimper, and I don't like the sound of that one bit.

As soon as she reaches the fence, I know she isn't going to stop. Sure enough, finding a toehold in the chain-link, and a grip with her good hand, Miss Milea climbs to the top and drops down on the other side. I cover my mouth in dread. I just cannot believe my teacher could be so reckless. She doesn't stop there, however, but darts for the closest building. The door is ajar, with lights on in one wing only. It's then I realize the scraping noise is coming from inside. With a start, I see someone cross the window dressed in butchers' aprons and another figure behind him in the same garb. I realize it is this one who is behind the noise. I watch him sharpening his knife on a whetstone, and remind myself to keep breathing.

"Come back," I plead, in a voice so faint that it barely escapes my lips. "Please don't go further!"

Miss Milea mounts the step in front of the building, either unaware or unconcerned by the activity. Next she eases herself through the gap in the door, and disappears from sight.

At once Solace strains to be released from my grip, but I dare not let her go. I look down, bidding her to be still, and see the last watt of light leave my head torch. Even as I slip the device from my head to see if I can tap some life into it, I hear murmuring from the poultry farm. I look up, just as two stocky figures emerge from the building.

Immediately, I pull Solace low and plead with her to stay quiet. When I dare to peep out once again, I see the men standing on the step, cast in silhouette by the lamplight. They talk in low voices, grumbling about this and that, but I'm too far away to make out what they're saying.

"Miss Milea," I whisper to myself. "What have you done?"

Perhaps Solace understands me, because she bristles at this and growls. I throw a finger to my lips, glaring at her to stay quiet, but I fear it is too late.

*"Who's there?"* I hear one of the butchers call out. *"I swear I just heard something!"*

With my back pressed to the twisted trunk, I steal

a glance in their direction. Both men have moved off from the step now, silent as they strain to listen. My knees feel like they can't support me, and my stomach shrinks to a ball. I grasp Solace's muzzle as the snarl builds in her throat, grimacing at the noise.

"*Listen!*" one butcher hisses to the other. When he turns around to face the open door, I realize with a start that it isn't my presence he's picked up on. "An intruder!"

Without word, both butchers charge inside. They practically fight with each other to be first to get their frames through the door. All I can do is watch in horror, knowing who is in there. I want to scramble over the chain-link fence and rescue her, but the sound of crashing pots and voices raised in surprise and then anger roots me to the spot.

Next I hear a scream. This time, I know just who it belongs to, because I have heard it once tonight already.

In response Solace launches from our hiding place. I haul her back by the collar, my blood curdling, for a silence has returned as swiftly as it had been smashed. I see shadows sweep across the rear walls in the building, and movement on the grassland. It is to the burrows that I turn my attention, for the biggest rabbit I have ever seen emerges under the stars. It isn't just the creature's body that is bloated. Its bloodshot eyes look fit to pop from their sockets. This is what finally tips me into turning tail, urging my dog to run with me.

"Let's get out of here," I cry, and sprint once more into the woods. With Solace, I am sure that I can make it through without my head torch. It can't be more frightening than this. I don't want to think that I am abandoning Miss Milea. Nor do I want to consider what else I am leaving behind. For as soon as I flee the poultry farm and the surrounding burrows I hear a gruesome noise indeed. It is not the sound of butchery, but a soft, squelching explosion followed by a brief pattering over the ground.

# 13

Overnight, a dense fog has settled over the community. It feels as if it has crept in through the lanes from all sides, consuming us while we were sleeping.

Through my bedroom windowpane, the summit of the scarp appears to be floating freely. From the back gate, the view of the meadow and the woods has disappeared entirely. In some ways I wish it would vanish for real. Even Solace seems to share my feelings. I crept downstairs before dawn to take her back and forth across the meadow. Instead of turning circles restlessly until I had hauled on my walking boots, she remained on the tiles and refused to move.

I suggested we head for the old green instead.

Solace simply looked up at me with those sad brown eyes of hers. Under normal circumstances, I might have feared that my dog was ill. In view of what we had witnessed, I understood her reluctance to go out.

Last night, as we fled the woods, nothing blocked our path. We simply ran right over the point where that awful raven corpse had been left. For much of the night I thought about Miss Milea. A sense of guilt and dread stopped me from sleeping until the early hours. Endlessly, that bloodcurdling scream played out in my mind. I kept telling myself that no harm could possibly have come to her. She had not trespassed with any sense of malice. Our crime had been curiosity, though this did little to calm my fears. All I could do was twist and turn with my poor teacher in my thoughts.

Finally, when my lids grew heavy and closed, I dreamed of rabbits.

Come daylight, I clung to some doubts. I had certainly seen a bloated bunny, but I did not actually *witness* it burst into little bits. I knew what I had heard, but it proved nothing, and with that I began to question whether I had leapt to conclusions about Miss Milea. Desperate to find myself mistaken, I reasoned that people shrieked for lots of different reasons. As hard as I tried, however, I just could not escape from the belief that she had sounded terrorized.

ANALYSE DREAMS

♦ 💀 ♦

At breakfast my mother does not need to ask me if I am troubled. First I had abandoned Solace's walk, and now my loss of appetite speaks volumes.

"You haven't eaten a spoonful, Kamil. What is wrong?"

I am facing an egg that she has boiled for me. When I look up from it, I find her gazing right into my eyes. She has brushed her white hair through, but has yet to pin it up for the day. Every time I come downstairs in the morning she is here, with a shawl thrown around the shoulders of her night-gown, though I never once hear her rise before me. My mother could pass over creaking floorboards and they would never make a sound.

"I'm just not hungry," I say, and push the egg cup across the table.

"Then give it to Solace," she replies. "We can't afford to waste a scrap."

The dog is at my feet, resting on her front paws. Again, her eyes tell me everything.

"She's off her food as well," I say. "Why don't you have it?"

My mother draws the chair back from the table. "Very well," she says, sitting before the egg cup. "It's from old Wenzel. He knocked on our door yesterday and invited me to pick an egg from a tray."

"Wenzel?" I say in disbelief. "But it's not in his

82

nature to be kind to anyone!"

"I couldn't believe it myself. He claims his hens have started laying like there's no tomorrow and he doesn't want them to go rotten. He's handed out eggs to half the community, so he told me." She pauses there and holds my attention. "He might be difficult, Kamil, but in lean times we do our best for one another."

I watch my mother take a spoon and break the crown of the shell.

"We need to build you up," I say, hoping to brighten the tone. "People have started to say you really ought to put some meat on your bones."

My mother freezes, with her spoon poised before her mouth.

"What people?"

"Cosmina Barbescu," I say, rather wishing I had kept quiet. "Mister Petri, too."

Nodding quietly to herself, she continues to eat.

"Cosmina has a pointed opinion about everyone," she tells me. "The way she's been moaning about the noise old Wenzel's chickens make, I very much doubt he graced *her* with a spare egg. As for Mister Petri, I don't have a bad word to say about him, and nor should you. I appreciate his concern for me, but you can tell him I'll survive on what rations he can provide. Worse things have happened to this family, as you well know."

I watch my mother scoop out one spoonful of egg yolk after another. Before my father vanished, she always had such rosy cheeks at any time of day. Now, shadows hang under her eyes from dawn to dusk, and though she eats from time to time it just does not seem to nourish her. Despite her decline, I think, she will always be my mother. Someone I should be able to confide in, come what may.

"Can I talk to you about something?" I ask, and prepare to tell her about Miss Milea.

"Not when this week's provisions are waiting to be collected," she says, and offers me a rare smile. "If you must skip breakfast, then go now and you won't be last in the queue again!"

# 14

After everything that has happened, facing
Mister Petri is the last thing I want to do. It is also
something I cannot avoid. If I don't pick up the food
parcel from him then we will go hungry.

I am by no means near the front of the queue.
Every week, as desperation grows, people arrive earlier and earlier. As it is, the fog is just so thick this
morning that I can barely see the back of the truck.
Thanks to the vehicle's rear lights, I can make out
Mister Petri's tall, wiry frame. He's in high spirits as
he hands down box after box. I hear him chatting
and chuckling as he works, which makes me wonder
if he is even aware of what happened at the Squawk
Box last night. His sons flank the truck. They stand

in leather coats with their shaven skulls exposed to the cold. Barely blinking, they observe each villager who steps up to be served. As we move forward, I feel my heart race. I just do not know how I will be able to look their father in the eye.

"*Good morning, my sweet! How are you? And the little ones? Bless them!*"

I cannot see who Mister Petri is greeting. Cosmina Barbescu is among those who have arrived before me. Even though she is astride her mobility scooter today, her huge girth blocks my view. Judging by the racket from old Wenzel's hens, however, I have a hunch that she is snacking from her basket while she waits to be served.

"*Do pass on my regards to your family. Now, who is next?*"

Obediently, accompanied by the whine of the mobility scooter, we all shuffle forward. I am one step closer to facing Mister Petri. For a moment, I wonder whether he is perhaps addressing Flori. I strain to see, hoping that my friend really has just suffered nothing more than a winter cold, but the fog and Cosmina conspire to obscure my view. I can't help thinking that if it is Flori then she might by now be as bloated as the bunny. I picture her reaching up for her weekly provisions looking swollen and ever so sorry for herself. It isn't something I wish to dwell upon, however, and so I tell myself that nobody would ever show their face in such a condition. It would cause panic, and right now the mood here is one of quiet irritation at the din from the chickens.

"*There you go. Look after yourself, now. Eat well, won't you?*"

I step forward as the next person takes their turn in front of the truck. At the same time, the figure who has just received the food parcel from Mister Petri breaks away from the queue.

I watch her hurry away with her head bowed, and blink before I can speak.

"Miss Milea?" It comes out as a whisper. So I clear my throat and call across so loudly that everyone turns to face me. "Miss *Milea!*"

# 15

I am not mistaken. My teacher looks around when I call out to her again. She is clutching her parcel against her chest. As soon as she sees me her face tightens. For a moment I think she is close to tears. She draws breath to say something, but thinks better of it and retreats into the fog.

Straight away I think I should run after her. Then I consider the queue behind me. If I lose my place I'll be late for school, and that's where she must be heading now. The queue moves up once more. I step forward like everyone else, elated at seeing Miss Milea alive and well. I am coming ever closer to being served by Mister Petri, but now I cannot stop smiling to myself. Such is my joy, I am the last to notice that the individual at the head of the line is the subject of much muttering.

As old Wenzel receives his provisions for the week, it is Cosmina Barbescu who is the most vocal.

"That's a generous parcel," she suggests to those within earshot. Cosmina is careful not to speak up so loudly that Mister Petri will hear, but she has the attention of everyone around her. "That's a very generous parcel indeed!"

The package that Mister Petri hands down doesn't really look much bigger than any other. Even if Cosmina is simply peeved because Wenzel's poultry have picked up on her eating habits, her comments prompt everyone to watch the old man depart.

"Move now," he grumbles to nobody in particular, and attempts to tuck his parcel inside his ragged coat. The scowl on his face looks like it has been in place for years. It crinkles his brow and leaves his eyes pinched tight at the corners. I even wonder if he sleeps with the same expression. "Let me through!"

"Maybe when you get home you'll discipline your chickens," Cosmina calls after him. She pauses there to chew down whatever she has been eating. Immediately, the background clucking calms. "That's what they need. *Discipline*."

This time, Mister Petri hears her loud and clear. She is now just one person away from being served. When she does pull up at the front of the queue she finds him gazing down at her with a look of wry amusement.

"You can't discipline a chicken, Cosmina. They need tender love and care."

"Old Wenzel's hens are out of control," she tells him from her pilot's seat. "They're picking on me."

"Maybe they're trying to tell you something." Mister Petri collects another food parcel from the shelf. "A hen will stop eating when she's full. It doesn't matter what delights you scatter for her, if she's had enough she'll ignore it."

"Oh, I'll stop when I'm full as well," Cosmina replies as Mister Petri drops the parcel into her basket. "Of *course* I'll stop! It's just I'm always hungry."

Mister Petri dusts his palms and then rolls up his shirtsleeves. "That should see you through the week, my girl. You won't get peckish there."

I see Cosmina lean forward and take a peek inside the parcel.

"I might go hungry before old Wenzel," she complains.

I wince as she says this. Indeed, several people in front of me attempt to shuffle backwards. Even Mister Petri's sons glance at their father to see how he might respond.

"Old Wenzel received a little something from me because I heard about his act of generosity," he says, speaking in a low voice now. "He might be an old billy goat, Cosmina, but he gave away his eggs yesterday and that should be rewarded."

"He didn't knock on *my* door," she points out.

This time Mister Petri's expression darkens considerably. He strokes the whiskers protruding from his great chin, studying Cosmina first and then each of us in the queue behind her.

"Fortunately," he says finally, "I have enough provisions on board to provide a treat for you all." With that, he returns his attention to Cosmina. "Would you care for an extra tin of treacle pudding?"

"Bless you!" Cosmina squeals. "An extra tin of *treacle pudding*!"

With the offering safely stowed in her basket, she grasps the steering column and peels her scooter around in reverse. The vehicle moves much faster backwards. It causes those behind her to sidestep

out of her way. Then, sitting upright in her seat, with her feet planted squarely upon the footplate, she crawls forward without a parting glance at any of us. Mister Petri's sons watch her leave, narrowing their gaze as this moving mountain on wheels makes her way through the mist.

The space she leaves behind takes several steps for everyone in the queue to fill. Mister Petri works swiftly now to meet each reaching pair of hands. Indeed, it is only a matter of minutes before I find my turn has come. I take a deep breath, move forward and face up to him.

Mister Petri studies me closely, and then nods to himself. For one awful moment I think he must know that I have been making a nuisance of myself around the poultry farm. Since I have seen him serve Miss Milea, however, I see no reason why he should be sharp with me.

"How is your mother?" he asks at last. "Is she eating?"

"She enjoyed old Wenzel's egg," I tell him.

"And Solace?" he asks. "Such a formidable dog."

"Solace is off her food," I say in all truth, though immediately I wish that I had kept that to myself.

"The poor creature. What is wrong? I trust you haven't let her venture anywhere near the rabbits around my farm? Things are becoming dire for those burrows. Only this morning I found the remains of one poor bunny. Whatever has caused this lethal bloating, it's bursting them at the seams."

I sense my mouth go dry, forcing me to swallow. "Solace just doesn't much like the darker months," I say. "I'm sure she'll get her appetite back."

"I'm sure she will," Mister Petri agrees, and immediately heads for the shelves inside his truck. "Here," he says, bringing something wrapped in greaseproof paper. "It's one of the finest battered sausages a dog could ever taste. The batter is made with beer and a pinch of curry powder. If this doesn't put some life into her, nothing will."

I accept the treat politely, and collect the parcel he hands down to me. I turn to leave, only to pause and face back to Mister Petri. I think I might brave asking him what is happening at the Squawk Box. All of a sudden, I feel compelled to do so. Then I sense his sons are glaring at me, and what little pluck I have found just melts away.

Solace watches me place the box of provisions on the kitchen table. She has yet to lift her muzzle from her front paws. I see my mother has placed some broken-up biscuits in her bowl, but they have not been touched.

"I have something for you," I say, and take the wrapped treat from my pocket. "Something fresh and tasty."

Her nose twitches as I wave it in front of her. At the same time, my mother appears at my side.

"You're in good spirits, Kamil. What was troubling you at breakfast that you wanted to speak to me about?"

I think about Miss Milea, and smile to myself.

"Oh, I thought I had lost something," I tell her. "I was wrong."

My mother looks at me, waiting for more details, but I don't wish to do that now. Miss Milea would have all the answers I needed about the poultry farm, and I intended to talk to her after class. In a bid to break her gaze, I show my mother the battered sausage. She brightens when I hand it to her.

"How kind of Mister Petri." Peeling apart the wrapping, she draws the crispy-covered delicacy close to her nostrils. "Freshly prepared, too. What a rare treat!"

"He suggested that I feed it to Solace."

By now, the dog is up on her feet and swishing her tail from side to side. A little drool forms in the corner of her jaws. If she had lost her appetite, she has certainly found it now.

"Why don't you have half yourself?" my mother suggests. "It's too good to give the whole thing to the dog."

I look at Solace. I know she can't understand what's just been said, but she's so locked on to the slightest change in mood that she must know why I'm hesitating. She whines pleadingly when I reclaim the sausage from my mother. I am hungry now, I realize. It's been so long since I chewed on fresh-cooked meat. The stuff that comes out of the tins just isn't the same. It has no bite. No *flavour*.

"Solace," I say eventually, and drop the battered delight into her bowl. "As much as I would enjoy it, this is Mister Petri's gift to you."

The dog's jaws fall upon the sausage. Despite an unexpected crunch, she wolfs it down in seconds. As she does so, I hear hens squawk and cluck. This time, it isn't just coming from the direction of old Wenzel's cottage. The noise has struck up from coops all around the community. It doesn't last long, and when peace sets in once more I wonder if I had imagined it. My mother doesn't even appear to have noticed. She's just watching Solace lick her black lips clean.

"Let's hope she doesn't expect this every day," she says, and begins to unpack the tins.

I think about this. "Do you believe the lean times will ever end?"

My mother stacks the cupboard shelf, her back turned to me. "When your father went missing, I spent every day for a year believing that he would return."

"And now?" I ask when she falls quiet.

"Now I just accept that this is how it will be."

"I still hope one day he'll appear," I say after a moment.

My mother faces me. Her eyes are shining. I know that I should leave for school now, if only so she can cry.

"Too much hope can be unhealthy, Kamil. If it leaves you feeling disappointed, you have to let it go."

# 17

In class, Miss Milea instructs us to follow exercises from our school books. She keeps us so quiet throughout the day that it feels like we are sitting for surprise examinations. As we study, she remains behind her desk and marks our work with her good hand. We cover every subject, but I cannot concentrate. I keep looking up, hoping to catch her eye. Every time, I find her looking utterly lost in thought.

Towards the end of the school day, I wonder whether our teacher is with us at all.

The desk beside me remains empty. I had hoped to find Flori here when I arrived. Her absence makes me worry, though I hold out hope that she is simply suffering from a seasonal ailment. Once again, Mister Petri had spoken darkly of a mortal bloat among the rabbits. Until I speak to Miss Milea, however, and find out what happened inside the Squawk Box, I am not sure whether I should believe him. I think about this with my attention fixed on the tree line beyond the cottages and shacks. I used to consider the woods as a place where I could leave my worries behind. Now, it has become the source of them.

"Kamil? Have you completed the exercise?"

I am startled to hear Miss Milea break the silence.

"Not yet," I say, turning quickly from the window.

"Then you don't have time to daydream." Her manner is clipped and fierce, which is unlike her. She is sitting upright behind her desk, barely blinking as she addresses me. "Everybody else has been working hard. It seems you are the last to finish, in fact."

I look around, and see that my classmates are sitting patiently with their exercise books closed.

"I didn't realize," I say weakly.

Miss Milea glances at the clock on the wall. The cowbell isn't due to ring for another five minutes. She purses her lips for a moment, the silence broken only by the ticking minute hand, and then dismisses the class.

"Please stay behind until you have completed your work," she instructs me, raising her voice as my classmates rush for the door.

I hold back a smile. Clearly Miss Milea is as keen as I am to talk. I wait for the last pupil to leave, and then rise to my feet.

"I've been so worried," I say. "What happened to you last night?"

Miss Milea remains in her seat, her bad hand tucked out of sight as usual. As I approach the front of the classroom her eyes pinch at the corners.

"I asked you to stay behind to work, Kamil. Please return to your desk."

I halt in my tracks, puzzled and a little alarmed.

"But we need to talk!"

"There is nothing more to say. What occurred last night is in the past. I do not wish to speak about it ever again." All of a sudden, a hint of fear comes into her voice. "Please," she says. "Cast it from your mind and promise me you'll never again go near the Squawk Box."

I listen to what she says feeling shocked and numb. It's as if the Miss Milea who disappeared into the poultry farm has come out a different person.

"Are you OK?" I ask quietly. "Is everything all right?"

101

In response my teacher gathers her books with her good hand and rises from her seat.

"No," she says plainly. "Everything is not all right."

I do not have to ask her any more questions. Even if I wanted to, I would fail to find the right words. For as she stands, I see that her bad hand is bandaged to the wrist. It's a little bloodstained too: a coin-sized crimson stain where I'm sure one of her remaining fingers should be.

In that instant, I gather my breath as if surfacing from a spell underwater. For not only am I sure Miss Milea has lost another digit at the hands of those menacing butchers, I fear I know where it ended up.

"Solace," I say to myself, thinking back to the moment my dog devoured that battered treat. "Solace, what have we done?"

I focus on Miss Milea. Tears gloss her cheeks now. She wipes them dry with the sleeve of her good arm, and tells me to leave my finished work on her desk. "Do the best you can, Kamil. Perhaps one day you'll have the knowledge to help us all get away from here."

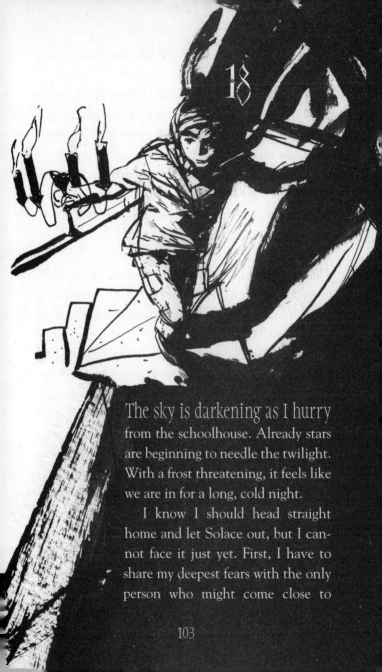

The sky is darkening as I hurry from the schoolhouse. Already stars are beginning to needle the twilight. With a frost threatening, it feels like we are in for a long, cold night.

I know I should head straight home and let Solace out, but I cannot face it just yet. First, I have to share my deepest fears with the only person who might come close to understanding me. I just hope that she'll be in a fit state to listen.

I knock several times at Flori's front door. Nobody answers. I venture into the yard to see if I can find her father, only to discover that his flock have already taken to their roost. Every keeper in the community makes sure their birds are in a safe place before the light fades. Poultry do not like to be outside after dark, after all. A chicken is born knowing it is easy meat. This is an instinct that serves to help it live another day.

As we are only on the cusp of night, however, I cannot tell whether Flori's father has encouraged his hens in early for their own safety, or if they retreated by their own will.

Not wishing to alert the birds to my presence and risk another song and dance, I return to the front and call out Flori's name. Her curtains are closed, and do not twitch. I bite my lip, concerned. Could she be stranded in her bed? Too inflated by gases to stand? It is then that I decide to let myself in. I know the door will be open. Nobody ever feels the need to lock up in this small community. We are not under threat like the chickens. At least, we weren't until now.

"Flori? Hello? It's me. Kamil." I climb the staircase, causing every step to creak. It is so gloomy that I take a candelabrum from the dresser at the top and light all four wicks. Shadows flicker across the walls as I turn to find her room. The door is ajar. I knock quietly. "May I come in?"

I wait for an age for an answer, and then steel myself for the worst. I take a breath before opening the door. When I lay eyes on my friend, I am unsure what I have found. Flori is propped up on pillows with her eyes closed and hands clasped over the sheets. She looks so pale and at peace that at first I think I am too late. Then she blinks and looks quite relieved to find me at the foot of the bed.

"Another bad dream," she says. "I'm glad you woke me."

"How are you?" I ask, feeling very awkward all of a sudden. I am also unsure if I should move any closer. Flori doesn't look at all puffed up, though I flinch when she reaches for a handkerchief to blow her nose.

"Mostly, I feel like that raven is haunting me," she says, sounding croaky as she finds her voice. "Every time I close my eyes I see the four chicken skulls strapped to its back. I even dream that they speak to me."

"What do they say?"

"That I should never step foot in the woods again."

I place the candelabrum on her dressing table, and take myself to the high-backed chair in the corner.

"We should heed their warning." I rest my elbows on my knees and look to the floor for a moment. Before I can tell her about Miss Milea, I know I shall have to confess to venturing back to the poultry farm once more. "Flori, since you fell ill some bad things have happened."

With great effort, Flori draws herself into a sitting position. "Go on," she says, and promptly sneezes into her handkerchief.

# 19

Throughout my account, Flori listens without word. She speaks only when I reach my conviction that Mister Petri had treated my dog to something so ghastly I can barely find the words.

"Please," she says, and shows me her palm. "Stop there, Kamil."

I am relieved that I do not have to continue. Looking at Flori, I believe she has already concluded that Mister Petri fed Solace that finger as a chilling way of warning me to stay out of his business.

"I'm scared," I say after a moment. "Not just for me any more. For the *community*."

She nods in understanding, and then turns her attention to the window.

Smoke rises from the chimneys of several cottages. On such a still night these silvery columns do not spread or drift. They clear the mountain scarp and simply wind into the void.

"If everything you say is true," says Flori, "then what is Mister Petri hiding from us?"

"Something terrible." This is all I can bring myself to say, but it is not enough for Flori. In the pause that follows, I can see from her changing expression that she is thinking things through.

"If there's a fresh demand for poultry products," she says next, "surely that marks an end to the lean times. It would be a cause for celebration among us."

"It would," I agree, rising to my feet. "But I do not believe the demand is for eggs and chickens."

"But what else can it be?"

As she asks me this, the candle flames gutter and bow. I turn to see Flori's father filling the door frame. He's wearing his coat, but removes his hat to greet us. On seeing his daughter sitting up in bed he smiles and sits at her side.

"I knew a good rest would help." He presses his

palm to her brow, and seems pleased by her temperature. "A good rest and hot elder tea. There's no better way to treat a winter cold. Isn't that right, Kamil?"

"Yes sir, it is," I say without hesitation.

"May I speak to you downstairs?" he asks. "My daughter needs peace and quiet now."

I glance at Flori. "It really is just a cold," she says, though I am unsure if she is playing it down for my benefit or for her father's.

The poacher takes the candelabrum with him, making sure that Flori is comfortable before closing her door. I head down the stairs first, aware that he is right behind me. Hanging his coat on the hook behind the front door, he invites me to follow him into the kitchen. Here, unlike any other cottage in the community, food can be found in abundance. All of it is wild, of course, and preserved or dried to see them through the winter months. Strings of mushrooms and garlic hang from the rafters overhead, ready to be used for anything from squirrel stew to pheasant casserole. On the shelves, bunches of nettle, elder, chickweed and marjoram sit alongside pots of chestnuts for roasting.

It is what's on the table that draws my attention, however. Piled on top of a chopping board, I count half a dozen dead sparrows.

Flori's father catches my eye. "When she's well again, my daughter will bake a fine pie with these. She's a gifted cook. Unlike her late mother, she knows how to bone a bird thoroughly so this family doesn't suffer another choking tragedy." He sets the candelabrum on the table, looking lost for a moment, then invites me to be seated. "Sparrow doesn't provide a great deal of meat, but with the right seasoning and a little lard it can be very satisfying. I bagged them in the woods as the sun was setting," he says, before clasping his hands and looking at me over the candle flames. "Near the poultry farm."

I can't help but glance at the sparrows. They don't appear to be bloated in any way. When I look back at Flori's father, I can tell that he knows just what I'm thinking.

"Last night," I say, and pause to find my voice, "I witnessed some frightening things at the Squawk Box. I know you warned me not to go there, but one thing led to another and—"

"The darkness can play tricks on your imagination," he says, stopping me in my tracks. "Working under the stars as I do, I have to question everything. What I see, or hear, is not necessarily what I believe it to be. What might sound like a bunny blowing into bits might just be a crab apple dropping from a branch into a bog."

"I know what I heard," I say firmly, sensing my frustration build. "Besides, this isn't just about the rabbits!"

"And I know what I heard on the day your father disappeared. Because this isn't just about Flori!"

The silence that follows is intense. I hadn't meant to raise my voice, and I doubted very much that the poacher had meant to say what he had in response. He looks surprised at himself, in fact, and I know why. He had replied in the heat of the moment, clearly tested in the first place by finding me confiding in his daughter. Despite it all, those words could not be taken back now.

"What can you tell me?" I ask eventually, and silently instruct myself to stay as calm as I can.

With a sigh, his broad shoulders sag. He looks to his hands for a moment, and then finds me through the candlelight once more. "I just know that Mister Petri is not someone you want to cross. He's a powerful man, Kamil. At any time he could choose

111

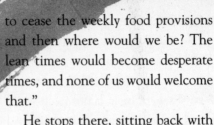

to cease the weekly food provisions and then where would we be? The lean times would become desperate times, and none of us would welcome that."

He stops there, sitting back with his arms folded.

I remain where I am. "I have good reason to believe Mister Petri is hiding something," I say. "And now I know that you are, too."

Flori's father flattens his lips. He rasps his unshaven chin with one hand, reflecting on things. Then he smiles despite himself. "You certainly have your father's determined spirit," he tells me. "In many ways it proved to be his undoing."

Hearing him say this makes me quiver inside, but I will not leave until I know more.

"I beg you," I say. "As his son, I deserve to know the truth."

By the time I return home, the
moon has climbed out from behind the
woods. I creep in through the back door,
hoping not to wake my mother. Solace
is there to greet me. As soon as I set eyes
on her, I think about poor Miss Milea. I
know the dog is not to blame for what happened,
but somehow she seems different to me now. I am
happy to pet her, but for once I feel uncomfortable
when she licks my face.

"If only you could talk," I say, dwelling on what
Flori's father has just told me.

"What would she say?"

My mother is standing at the foot of the stairs.

I think at first that I have woken her. Then I note that she is wearing the same nightdress and shawl as she was this morning, and decide she must have left her hair untied all day.

"Do you remember when Solace came out of the woods without my father?"

"How could I forget?" She heads for her chair by the wood burner. I follow her, but remain on my feet. "As soon as I saw her," she continues, "I knew that something was wrong. Your father called her Solace because she was always at his side when he needed her. She would never leave him unless a bad thing had happened."

She turns her attention to the burner. Behind the glass, the logs crackle and spark in the flames.

"If Solace could talk she would surely tell us."

"Of course," she replies. "But dogs cannot speak, Kamil, and so we will never know."

I feel my stomach tightening. I really should tell her what I learned from Flori's father. I just do not know how she will respond.

"What if someone else was in the woods when he disappeared," I say hesitantly. "Maybe they could tell us."

My mother seems surprised at the suggestion. Her eyes fix on mine, and then she chuckles to herself. It is not what I had hoped for. "Kamil, you really must let it go. Everything I said to you this morning about

114

the perils of clinging to hope is true. Can't you see what it did to me? Don't be afraid to move on. Be *fearless* like your father."

"Nothing scared him," I say.

"Nothing at all."

Behind me, Solace has begun to whine quietly to herself. It is like she understands that we have been talking about her old master. As it is, I know she is waiting to be walked.

"I had better go," I say to my mother.

"Try not to be afraid of the dark," she says. "I know it's been troubling you lately, but it's all in your imagination."

"There's only one thing that doesn't scare me right now," I say to myself, on stepping out under the stars. "And that's the truth."

I do not take my head torch. There is no need when all I intend to do is throw sticks for Solace on the green. I need the space to think, and at this very moment that is not something the woods or even the meadow can offer. On the way there, my dog pads alongside me. She stays unusually close, and even circles me protectively when I pause to tie a loose bootlace.

"Relax," I tell her. "No harm will come to us here."

As we approach the green, I wonder if my father

115

said much the same thing as they wound their way through the trees for his last time. This is not something I will ever learn, of course, but at least now I know more about where his final path took him.

On that day, Flori's father had set out to check his snares and traps. As he told me in his own words, he heard my father approaching, talking to Solace as he walked, and decided to lie low. As a poacher, so he said, the need to stay out of sight was second nature to him. And so he watched from near by as my father continued his walk along the path. He thought nothing more of it, until minutes later the sound of raised voices reached his ears. He had crept through the foliage, tracking the sound of this heated disagreement, until he spied the figures responsible.

"*Your father and Solace had reached the farm,*" he had revealed to me earlier. "*There, I saw him facing Mister Petri through the chain-link fence. From what I could hear, he was pressing your father to help him invent a way to pack in more poultry. Mister Petri was insisting that the surest way to keep the farm from going out of business was to process more chickens. Now, as everyone knows, your father was a man of principle. I heard him refuse outright, claiming that the welfare of the birds should be considered. Mister Petri looked none too pleased by this. He suggested to your father that he should at least inspect the sheds before he reached a decision that would surely cost the community dearly. So, while Solace was left to sniff around the burrows, that's exactly what he did. I watched your father walk around to the main gates, which was the last I ever saw of him.*"

The poacher's account had left me dumbstruck. It didn't solve the mystery of what had happened to my father, but knowing that Mister Petri was involved in some way made absolute sense to me. As soon as I had gathered my thoughts, I swore that I would do my very best to expose any wrongdoing. It was there, however, that Flori's father forbade me from doing just that.

"*Why do you think I have kept silent for all this time?*" he had asked, rising from his chair to make his point. "*Because if anyone crosses Mister Petri he* will simply shut off their supplies! I have a daughter to consider, Kamil, just as you must think of your mother. She is all you have left, after all."

# 21

I had departed from the poacher's cottage feeling trapped by such words of warning. Flori's father was right. I could not afford to confront Mister Petri, even if I was brave enough to do so. However, it didn't stop me burning up with anger at the thought that the poultry farm owner might have been involved in my father's disappearance.

As Solace and I cross the green to the leafless beech, I pick up the first stick I can find and throw it as hard as I can.

Solace leaps the stream, the water bright with the reflection of stars and the moon above. She is swift enough to catch the stick in the air, before bringing it back for me to hurl again. I do not take it from her jaws, however. Nor do I respond when she drops it at my feet and sits expectantly with her tail switching this way and that. Instead, my attention is directed at the activity in a cottage across the green.

The curtains are drawn across Cosmina Barbescu's kitchen window. Thanks to the oil lamp inside, however, her silhouette is clear to see. Clutching Solace's collar so she does not bolt, I creep behind the trunk of the beech and observe from there. It is unmistakably her. She's tucked in so tightly that her big belly folds over the top and bottom of the table.

Outside the cottage, a familiar truck is parked on the cobbles. It isn't just the vehicle that tells me the figure standing over her must be Mister Petri. It is the long neck atop narrow shoulders, the angular gait and swathe of retreating hair. I am so surprised to see him there that I just have to get a closer look. Without further thought, I brave running into the open and take cover behind the wheel arch of his truck.

Peeping out now, with Solace behind me, I find the window once again. His silhouette is still standing over hers, but it's what I hear that draws me closer. A gale of laughter from Cosmina, followed by mock protests.

"I really cannot manage another tin, Mister Petri. Not even another spoonful. Any more will repeat on me. As much as I adore your suet pudding, three tins are quite enough."

121

"Then how about something very special to wash it all down?"

Mister Petri produces a carton. With the corner ripped away, he waves it like a smelling salt under Cosmina's nose. On this still night, I hear her draw a long intake of air through the nostrils.

From the yard next door, old Wenzel's chickens begin to squawk and cluck.

"*Egg custard?*" she asks with a gasp. "Can it be so?"

He dips a finger inside the carton, and invites Cosmina to taste it for herself. "Egg custard with a pinch of nutmeg."

"You *spoil* me, Mister Petri."

"I certainly do," he replies, and offers another coated finger to her lips.

I can barely believe what I'm seeing. I have never known anyone receive such a treat. Even Solace looks on enviously, and she has tasted things today that really should have killed her appetite completely.

"Delicious!" reports Cosmina. "Delicious and *divine!*"

"Have some more." This time, Mister Petri tears the carton wide open. "You know you can't possibly resist."

"Oh, but I must," she protests weakly. "That would be greedy."

"Open wide, Cosmina," he coos, standing over

her now. "Let's not miss a drop."

Despite the fuss from the chickens next door, I
can't avoid hearing the glugging sound that follows.
I can even make out the rise and fall of Cosmina's
throat as she swallows it down, which leaves me
feeling a little bit sick. She keeps her head tipped
back as Mister Petri pours the last of the custard
into her gullet. He finishes with a flourish and nods
approvingly when she burps.

"That's the best I've ever tasted," she declares.
"I'm so full I might burst."

"Oh, don't do that," says Mister Petri with a
chuckle. "It's hard enough work having to scrape
up the bunnies every morning."

"If only folks knew how special it tastes—"

"Folks *won't* know," he cuts in abruptly. "Otherwise everyone will want the luxury goods, and there aren't enough to go round just yet."

"It's our secret," agrees Cosmina quickly.

"And that's how it must remain," replies Mister Petri, only this time he turns his chin towards the curtains. I try very hard not to think that he is addressing me, but freeze where I am nonetheless.

*"We should be going,"* I whisper to Solace.

I prepare to cross back to the beech tree, letting Solace race off ahead of me, and then freeze when the headlamps of the truck I'm hiding behind flash on and off.

It had not occurred to me that there would be anyone waiting for Mister Petri in the vehicle. I am on the driver's side, and can only guess that one of his sons is behind the wheel. Then, despite the constant clucking, I pick up on the sound of footsteps approaching the back of the truck and realize that his brother must be close by. I'm so frightened that I think my heartbeat might give me away. I can only see his boots under the vehicle, but I watch them move around to the passenger side and climb in. Then I hear Mister Petri at Cosmina's door.

"Sweet dreams, my dear."

"No doubt," she answers. "I always sleep well on a full stomach."

"And remember," he says, his voice hushed. "Do not breathe a word to anyone."

"Why would I do such a thing? The more people who know, the fewer treats there are for me!"

"Wise words, Cosmina. Good night now."

Mister Petri walks briskly towards the truck. He mutters to himself about the noise made by the hens, which has suddenly become more urgent. I shrink inside myself, wishing I hadn't ventured this far from the green. Solace is back at the stream, sniffing around at her own reflection in the water. If he sees my dog, he will wonder where I am.

Instead, he reaches the vehicle and takes his place beside his sons. I hear a few words exchanged between them before the engine turns over and rattles into life. When the truck draws away over the cobbles, I remain where I am for a moment, crouching in a veil of exhaust fumes with my hands clasped over my head. Then the chickens give up their protest, one by one it seems. But the silence does not last.

"Kamil?" This is the voice of Cosmina Barbescu. "What are you doing?"

I look up, feigning surprise. "Walking Solace," I say, and cringe because that doesn't sound good at all.

Cosmina is at her front door still. "Have you lost something?"

"Yes," I reply, brightening now. "My dog."

"Has she shrunk?"

"I mean her name tag," I lie. "It fell off her collar some days ago."

At the mention of her name, Solace trots across and licks my cheek. I stand sheepishly. Cosmina studies me intently.

"Don't lose your dog, Kamil. In these lean times, she's worth a lot to somebody."

"I won't," I say, retreating from her with Solace at my side. "I must go, Cosmina. I really need to catch up with someone."

"You should run!" she calls after me. "The exercise will do you both some good!"

I do not know what to make of the scene I have just witnessed. Mister Petri took great delight in feeding Cosmina, and she clearly revelled in his attention. I still feel shocked at how close I came to being caught snooping, but I cannot just head home and pretend it never happened. And so I do just as Cosmina suggested. I turn with Solace and hurry in the same direction as the truck. I can still hear it in the lanes, crunching through the gears.

In the dark, I judge what direction to take by the truck's headlamps. The glow from the dual beams can be seen gliding through one lane after the next. I am breathless by the time I catch sight of the rear brake lights. Solace and I barrel across the square where the old folk play chess each afternoon, then duck behind a water butt.

"No barking!" I instruct her. "Not even a whine!"

Up ahead, the truck has stopped in front of the gates to the service lane. When the poultry farm was in business, the workers would walk up this fenced path between the trees before each shift, and trudge back afterwards. I am told that Mister Petri's grand mansion is visible from there, set back in private woods that we cannot access. Right now, it seems he's heading for home. Mister Petri himself climbs out of the cab to unlock the gates. He walks around the front of the truck, which is when I order Solace to wait for me and seize the chance to find out for myself.

By the time Mister Petri has opened up, I am crouched once more on the blind side of the vehicle. As soon as the truck moves off, I am ready to pass inside and then hide behind the nearest tree. I ask myself what on earth I am doing. Even Solace is watching me with her head tipped to one side,

*where is my chart of the heavens?*

128

baffled by my actions.

As the vehicle slips through, I peel away and crash through bracken for cover. Keeping low there, I wait for the headlights to leave me in darkness.

Barely has the truck trundled off, however, when I sense something approach me from behind. I glance out, panic-stricken, upon which Solace pads through the gloom.

"I told you to stay!" I hiss, though I can never truly be cross with my dog. In all honesty I am pleased she has slipped through the gates to be with me.

At once, I feel an enormous sense of elation. I had not planned this, but it feels like the right thing to do. All day I had lived with the sense that shadows were gathering around our community, and now I had seized the chance to find out what was responsible.

Together with Solace, I wade through the bracken to the track. Behind us, the cottages and shacks beyond the gates look quite closed off from the world. The lights in the windows also make it seem like a warm and safe place to be. It is then I remind myself that I am not equipped with my head torch. Still, the night sky is milky with stars. Their light may not penetrate the woods that flank us, but I can at least see where I am going.

"This way," I tell Solace, anxious to catch up with the truck now.

When I break into a jog, my dog matches it effortlessly. Within minutes we have left the lights from the community behind. When I look back, I notice winter clouds gathering behind the scarp. Moonlight silvers their flanks, revealing them to be dense and billowing. If they creep overhead while I'm out here, I'll barely be able to see my own hands. With this in mind, as well as the sudden realization that I can no longer hear the truck's engine, I pick up the pace even more. The track follows a long but gentle bend, but all I can hear now are our own footfalls. Breathlessly I vow not to let myself be overtaken by fear. I can sense it catching up, which just serves to make me run faster.

It does not occur to me that the truck might have stopped. It is only when I bowl around the bend that I realize this is why the engine has died. By then, it is too late.

"Kamil. Now this is most unusual!"

Mister Petri is waiting for me, it seems. He's standing behind the truck with a son on either side. I pull up so smartly that I practically freeze on the spot. Solace lopes around me and buries her muzzle into his outstretched palm.

Mister Petri lifts his eyes to mine. With this stretch of track bathed in a red glow from the tail lights, I see him grinning broadly. "May I feed her another treat? She clearly has a taste for it."

Mister Petri's sons seem most amused by their father's offer. They even chuckle as he digs around inside the pocket of his overcoat.

"*No! Please!*" I raise my palms in protest, only to drop them quickly when I realize I am in no position to tell him what to do. "What I mean to say is, it isn't wise to feed a large dog straight after exercise. If she eats too fast it can cause her intestines to twist. It could kill her," I add, and then rather wish I hadn't.

In the pause that follows my outburst, Solace returns to my side. Mister Petri stops grinning. I realize he has no interest at all in Solace's welfare.

"Kamil, you are aware that this is trespass."

Nervously, I look to my feet for a moment.

"I am indeed," I say. "I'm sorry."

"Perhaps you should tell me what brings you here."

I face up to him again, but cannot find a way to begin.

"Is it the Squawk Box?"

At this, all I can do is nod guiltily. Solace must sense that I am uncomfortable. She looks up at me, flattening her ears. "Sir," I ask finally, "is it open for business again?"

I note Mister Petri's sons glance at one another, and then in some surprise at their father when he confirms that it is.

"I knew it!" I say under my breath.

"But not as you might imagine," he adds, raising one finger to make his point. "I think you'll be surprised."

His sons are looking mightily uncomfortable now. I too feel great unease. I really don't want to be here. It is dark and cold, and I feel like I am some way from home.

"What surprises me," I say, "is that you've kept it a secret from the community."

"Oh, but I must!" he declares, clearly relishing this exchange. He steps forward, and circles Solace and me with his hands clasped behind his back. "Kamil, if everyone knew what was happening at

132

the poultry farm, there would be uproar."

"Why would that be?" I ask, feeling sick to my stomach.

"What we've started up is very low-key. If we announced it, there simply would not be enough work to go round. The operation is very much a family affair, you see. The Squawk Box just didn't work out as an intensive poultry farm. Times change, as we know to our cost. Those easy markets have become much fussier about the kind of meat they like to eat. It all comes down to supply and demand, Kamil. Having identified the demand, I've adapted the farm to supply it." Mister Petri stops behind me. I sense him leaning in to find my ear. "We've gone *free-range*."

I catch my breath and face him side on. "You have?"

Mister Petri nods proudly. "An organic chicken farm is the future, Kamil. Birds reared with plenty of space to scratch around live happier lives. The end result is a better class of meat product, and one that commands a higher price. Of course, there are fewer chickens to send to market, but each one is worth much more than the battery variety. It means we can make a living for ourselves at least, and if the business grows then it can only benefit the community."

I think about this for a moment, struggling to take it all in.

"But where are the chickens?" I ask. "There's no sound of them up there."

Mister Petri brushes the bristles on his chin. He seems to be thinking things through.

"Would you care to see?" he suggests finally. "As you've come this far, perhaps we could give you a tour. I do so enjoy showing choice members of the community around. Boys, why don't we let Kamil ride in the back?"

At this, his sons turn to open up the truck. Mister Petri loops his hand around my upper arm, upon which panic sets in.

# 24

"I should like to go home!" I insist, wriggling free from his grip. "I really cannot accept your invitation."

Mister Petri frowns. He looks quite vexed with me all of a sudden, as if his patience has run dry. "Why ever not?"

I begin to back away, aware that his sons are following. "Mister Petri, I saw Miss Milea this morning. I know what happened to her."

"But she was trespassing, too! If you're foolish enough to wander into a room full of cutting equipment, Kamil, one only has to slip or trip for disaster to strike. That chain-link fence is there for a reason, as is the Grand Perimeter. Do I need to remind you that there are bears and wolves and lunatics out there? If anyone crosses over, I cannot be held responsible should the worst occur, and the same rule applies to my farm."

"But her finger," I sputter. "You battered her poor finger and fed it to my dog!"

Mister Petri turns his attention to Solace, looking taken aback now, and then laughs out loud. He looks to his sons, who share in his amusement.

"You should be very careful when you make such claims, Kamil," he says, on recovering his composure. "People will start to mistrust every word you say!"

"But I saw it with my own eyes!" I protest.

"And where is the evidence?"

I look at Solace. Her attention is locked on Mister Petri. Ignoring her, with his eyes narrowed, he awaits my answer.

"Please let me go home," I ask instead.

"Tour the Squawk Box with us first."

"I really mustn't—"

My protest falters as the dog at my side begins to growl. Her lips curl at the corner, revealing teeth like flints. It's enough to halt Mister Petri and his sons in their tracks.

"What's got into her?" asks Mister Petri.

I want to tell him that it must be something she ate, but don't wish to anger him further. "Solace is just being protective," I say. "I only have control

over her so long as I am safe from harm."

Mister Petri is silent until the low, menacing rumble ceases. Then he shrugs, and tells me I am free to go.

"I suppose we wouldn't want to worry your mother," he says. "It is getting late, after all."

"Thank you, sir."

I cannot wait to get away. I want to take flight, but know I should walk calmly. I have Solace at my side, after all. So I turn to depart, only to freeze when Mister Petri bids me farewell.

"Do pass on my regards to your mother, in fact. It's her we should be concerned for, after all. She's just so undernourished."

"My mother will survive," I say without facing him. "She has managed since my father disappeared."

"Quite so. The poor fellow. I fear we will never know what happened to him. Goodnight, Kamil. And should you change your mind about touring the Squawk Box, just say the word."

I continue to walk away, keeping Solace close. I am trembling now, but not just in fright. The encounter has left me feeling both frustrated and angry. I am surprised at how effortlessly Mister Petri has coaxed such fury in me. I have never known anything like it. Maybe I had been too scared to confront him directly about my father, but in truth this was no time for it. Not here in the service lane, deep in the woods after dark, so very far from home.

I am relieved to hear the truck pull away behind me. I glance over my shoulder just once, pleased to see the headlights advancing through the dark in the opposite direction. As I hurry back down the track, I begin to realize what a lucky escape I have had. Even if Mister Petri and his sons were running a free-range operation at the Squawk Box, the prospect of undertaking a tour in his company chills me to the marrow.

From the gates, I see that many of the lights in the community have gone out for the night. Overhead, those clouds have begun to fold in around the peak of the scarp. I feel like I am the last person awake, and I do not like that one bit.

"Let's go home," I say to Solace, and lift the rabbit wire that skirts the gates so she can slip through.

As we wind through the warren of lanes, I cannot shake off the sense that we are being watched. I keep looking around, feeling as if the darkness is closing in on me, but see no sign of life.

# 25

Snow falls overnight. On the cusp of dawn,
I awake to find the meadow covered in a thin white
blanket pricked by blades of grass. Beyond, the floor
of the woods has been sheltered from the downfall by
the tree canopy. In such a bleached-out landscape, it
seems like a separate world.

It isn't until I open my bedroom window that I
notice another change. Instead of breathing in fresh
wintry air, I screw up my nose at a terrible smell.
It is so bad that I retreat from the window, and

wonder out loud what could be
the cause. Even when I come to
walk Solace, with a scarf wrapped
around my face and nose, I have to
turn around as soon as we reach the
green. The stench is just sickening.

"Maybe someone has sprinkled
chicken fertilizer on the crops. You
know how many poultry owners like to
make the most of all those droppings."
This is my mother's opinion at breakfast.
Even though our doors and windows are

shut, the stink has crept inside. I look at the plate of beans she has placed in front of me, and feel queasy. With a day at school ahead of me, I force myself to eat. My mother sits with a glass of water and watches. She finished a whole egg yesterday, and I know from experience that she will not eat again for some time.

"Chicken fertilizer can be unpleasant," I say between mouthfuls, "but this is like nothing we have known before. Besides, only a miracle will make those pumpkins grow."

My mother nods and sips from her glass. I want to tell her about everything that had happened to me yesterday. I just don't know where to start.

"What is on your mind?" she asks. "You look troubled, and so does your dog."

Solace is lying on the mat beside the back door. Her ears spike on hearing her name, but she doesn't lift her muzzle from her paws.

"She certainly looks off colour," I say, and wonder if Mister Petri's treat from yesterday really had disagreed with her. Then I worry that she'd been chasing rabbits, which just serves to remind me how much is on my mind right now. From the raven to Cosmina and the visit she had received, to Miss Milea, my father's disappearance and the mystery of what was happening at the Squawk Box. It was all beginning to feel like too much for me to investigate alone.

I look up at my mother, still reluctant to involve

her in all this, and feel only relief on hearing a knock at the door.

"Hey!" I say, surprised to see who is outside. I swing open the door, forgetting about the stench for a moment, and grimace at poor Flori.

"Is that any way to greet a friend?" she asks, and steps inside.

Flori has her nose pinched between two fingers. She waits for me to close the door behind her and then breathes out with a grin. Her cheeks are rosy from the cold and her eyes are clear blue and sparkling. She pops off her woolly hat. I have never seen her look so healthy.

Without thinking, I hug her warmly.

"I've been so worried," I say. "I thought you'd caught something bad from the rabbits."

Flori eases herself from my embrace. "Kamil, that's nonsense and you know it! Mister Petri just made it up to scare you from the Squawk Box."

"I'm not so sure." I glance over my shoulder. My mother is within earshot, but busy clearing the table. "I told you, I believe I heard one *explode* the other night."

Flori meets my eyes. "Have you been back to the poultry farm?"

"Let's talk on the way to the schoolhouse," I suggest quietly. "I have so much that I need to tell you."

We are not alone in finding the stink quite offensive. As we make our way through the lanes, everyone we pass has covered their noses.

I cannot work out where it is coming from. It does not get better or worse as we walk. It simply lingers, suffocating our community.

"We must pray for a breeze," suggests Flori. "A breath of fresh air!"

Having just shared my encounters, discoveries and suspicions with my friend, I had expected her to respond more constructively than this. The odour is certainly unpleasant, but what I have just told her is more pressing.

"You don't believe me, do you?" I ask.

Flori catches my eye. "I know you're not lying to me, Kamil. You are an honest boy, as everyone knows. I just think perhaps you're assuming the worst about everything. If Mister Petri catches you poking your nose into his business again he could cut your provisions without notice."

In class that day, Miss Milea is not herself again. Her bad hand remains bandaged and at every moment she attempts to keep it hidden. At the first glimpse, I offer Flori a knowing look. She glances at me uneasily, but focuses on the rest of the lesson.

By the time the school bell rings, dusk is beginning to close in. My classmates rush for the door and the yard outside, which only serves to inform us that the bad smell has yet to clear.

"Maybe something has died," suggests Flori as she packs her books away. "Something that's decomposing."

I am watching Miss Milea when she says this. My teacher turns from wiping down the blackboard and cautions us both to wait for a wind to blow. "It's best we just put up with it. Nature will take its course."

"But why?" I am puzzled by her reluctance. "If we

145

Poor M.M!

can find the source then perhaps we can stop it."

"It *cannot* be stopped," she says sharply, and then seems to remind herself to stay calm. "Please, Kamil, promise me you'll keep to your own affairs. Just go home, close the door behind you and stoke the wood burner. It's the only way to get through these dismal nights."

Outside the schoolhouse, covering our mouths and noses with our sleeves, I ask Flori if she believes me now. "Miss Milea is scared. Whatever happened to her at the poultry farm has turned her into a frightened mouse. She's scared of *everything!*"

"Maybe she lost her finger in another accident, as Mister Petri claimed."

We crunch through the snow at a brisk pace, anxious to be out of the stench.

"You're fooling yourself," I tell her. "And you know it."

Flori curls her lower lip, but keeps her eyes fixed on the snowbound cobbles ahead. "What I don't understand," she says eventually, "is why Mister Petri should be so secretive about going organic. And if he is responsible for Miss Milea's missing finger, accidental or otherwise, why go to such drastic lengths to keep people away? Everyone in the community is grateful for the provisions he supplies. They don't expect to earn a living from him, too. Not any more."

I have no answers for her, though I am aware the light is fading. "Flori, would you mind walking Solace with me to the green this evening? I really would appreciate the company."

Even with her mouth covered, I can see from the way her eyes pinch at the corners that she is grinning.

"Just as long as we don't go into the woods," she says.

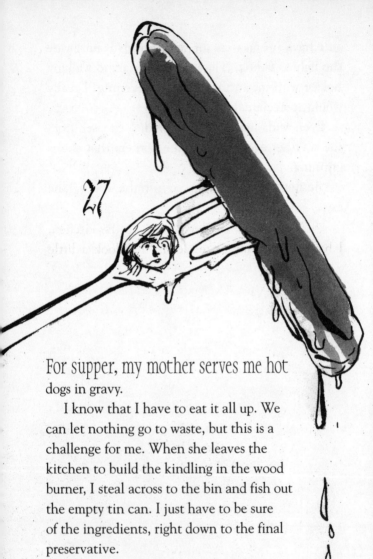

**27**

For supper, my mother serves me hot
dogs in gravy.

I know that I have to eat it all up. We
can let nothing go to waste, but this is a
challenge for me. When she leaves the
kitchen to build the kindling in the wood
burner, I steal across to the bin and fish out
the empty tin can. I just have to be sure
of the ingredients, right down to the final
preservative.

Even with my mind at rest, I cannot
begin to lift my knife and fork without

sending out Solace to join my mother. Every time I look at my dog, I am reminded of poor Miss Milea, and what she lost at the Squawk Box.

Gingerly, I prick the first hot dog with my fork. A greasy liquid bubbles out and slides into the gravy. Closing my eyes now, I take my first mouthful. There is little bite to it, and so I decide the best way to get it over and done with is to eat as fast as I can.

By the time my mother returns to the kitchen, I have scraped my plate clean. "You look a little green," she says. "What is wrong?"

"Nothing," I say. "Maybe some indigestion."

Outside, as I speak, Flori sweeps through the light from our kitchen window with her nose pinched once again. When I open the door to her, the first thing she does is hand me a greaseproof paper parcel tied up with string.

"A slice of sparrow pie," she says, stamping the snow from her boots. "My father said you might like to try it."

"Maybe later," I say, wishing I had held off eating supper now.

Flori looks over my shoulder. "Perhaps your mother should have it. It's still hot from the oven."

I turn to see my mother has taken to her chair by the wood burner. She is watching the kindling crackle and burn.

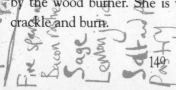

149

"Unfortunately, it is too late in the day for her. She never eats after dark. At this hour she just drifts into her memories." I place the parcel on the kitchen table, before crossing to fetch my head torch. "I really need to walk off my supper," I tell Flori. "Shall we go?"

Snow is falling outside. It tumbles out of the darkness, thick as goose down.

I am wrapped up against the cold like Flori. We have both pulled our scarves up around our noses. We agree that the stink has grown a little worse over the course of the day. I cannot imagine how intense it must be for Solace. As soon as we leave the cottage, she plants her nose to the ground with interest. On reaching the green, however, she pads around looking a little bit lost.

"What's wrong with her?" asks Flori. "Is she looking for something?"

This morning, we had barely made it this far. I just couldn't handle the smell, and had called my dog back to go home. Right now, I can only think my nostrils might have grown used to it. For a moment we watch Solace searching. She hunts full circle around the great beech, before returning with an air of defeat about her.

"Let's head back," I suggest. "If Solace doesn't want to be here then neither do I."

As soon as we turn, my dog slips around us to lead the way. It's as if she cannot wait to get home. As Flori and I feel the same way, we break into a jog behind her. By the time my cottage is in sight, I see her leap the gate and paw at the front door.

"Hey!" I call out, running towards her. "What's the hurry?"

As soon as my mother opens up, my dog slinks inside. "That was quick," she remarks, as we follow breathlessly behind.

A bark tells me where Solace has headed. I peer around the staircase and find her at the back door. She sees me watching her and wags her tail. I look back at Flori. She has just shut the front door against the stink. She pulls her scarf down to breathe freely, and then sees for herself what I am thinking.

"No way," she says. "Solace should have spent more time on the green. The woods are out of bounds."

I have to fight to be heard over the whining that strikes up in response.

"Cosmina said a dog like this needs proper exercise," I say, with some resignation. "There is only one place I can do that."

"It's out of the question," replies Flori, as my mother switches her attention between us. "Do you never learn?"

Sensing the tension between us, my mother invites Flori to warm herself by the wood burner. I hold my friend's attention for a moment longer. Then, as if it pains me, I excuse myself to quickly recharge my head torch.

28

In darkness, the snow that has settled on the meadow looks like candle wax. It is no longer falling so heavily, and I sense it will soon clear completely. Solace waits until I've closed the gate behind me, and then bounds away. I cover my mouth with my scarf, take a deep breath through it, and set off into the night.

I will take her to the edge of the woods and back again. In the space of half an hour, we can cross enough times to tire her out. The question for me is whether I can stand the stink. I also question how long I am brave enough to be out here. Providing I keep out of the woods, I tell myself, all will be well.

Midway across the meadow, I am startled by a sound behind me. I spin around on hearing the squawk, followed by a flapping like some mechanical toy unwinding. I even duck on instinct as I hear it closing in on me. Then my head torch catches the cause, just as it wobbles and weighs overhead. It's a chicken, struggling to stay in the air. I track her in the beam of light, barely able to believe what I am seeing. All I can do is stand and blink as she clears the upper branches of the woods by a whisker, as if hauled into the night by a celestial thread.

The silence she leaves behind is broken by the sound of my gate creaking. I turn to see a figure trudging through the snow towards me, and smile to myself.

"I'm glad you changed your mind," I call across to Flori.

She's looking over my head, I realize, into the sky over the woods.

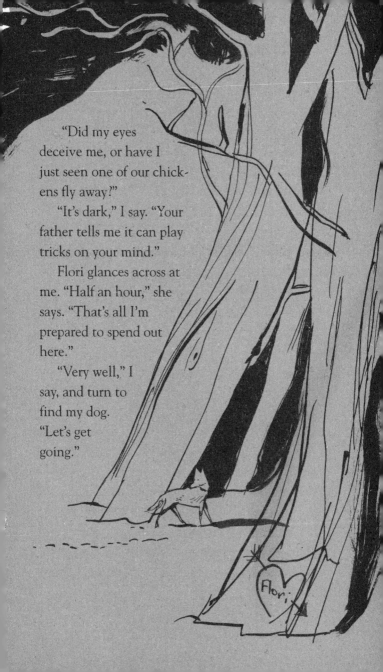

"Did my eyes deceive me, or have I just seen one of our chickens fly away?"

"It's dark," I say. "Your father tells me it can play tricks on your mind."

Flori glances across at me. "Half an hour," she says. "That's all I'm prepared to spend out here."

"Very well," I say, and turn to find my dog. "Let's get going."

It takes a moment to spot Solace. When I locate her, my smile shrinks away. She's waiting for me at the mouth of the woods, at the point where the dead raven had been planted. I whistle for her to come back. She barks at me.

"I'll fetch her," I say with a sigh.

"We'll both go," insists Flori.

Solace doesn't move when I call to her again. It's only when I'm close enough to reach her collar that she ducks from my grasp.

"What's wrong?" I ask, and remove my scarf so I can address my dog clearly. As soon as I do so, I realize that the stink is much stronger in the woods, just as Flori finds out for herself.

"Yuck!" She quickly covers her nose. "It's definitely coming from in here somewhere."

"I suppose the trees keep out the breeze," I say, facing back to her. "It's really stewed in here."

Despite the gloom, Flori looks around. Just as the trees have stifled any air movement, so the tangle of boughs and branches overhead has stopped much of the snow from reaching the floor of the woods. Instead, it slides free in clumps. In the darkness, it sounds like birds falling dead from their perches.

"OK," says Flori, trying hard to sound upbeat while retreating by a step. "So we know that something in the woods is to blame for the stink. Can we please go now?"

"Aren't you curious?" I turn to find Solace in the beam from my head torch. She's waiting impatiently some distance ahead. I also can't ignore what lies at the far end of the path. My head tells me to steer well clear. It also whispers to me that I should investigate a little further. "We could just go as far as the poultry farm."

"You and the dog are as bad as each other," replies Flori. "I know what you're thinking, Kamil. But even if the smell is coming from the Squawk Box, you don't have enough charge in your torch to see you to the chain-link fence and back."

I think about this for a moment. "We would if we ran home afterwards!"

"This isn't child's play, Kamil. The last time we came back from the poultry farm it felt like we were fleeing for our lives!"

"*Something* up there is rotten," I reply urgently. "Now is the time to find out."

For a moment, Flori seems torn by indecision. Then she sighs, as if pained by the choice she has made.

I grin at her as she joins me.

# 29

Without word, we follow the light from my head torch. I keep it trained on Solace's hindquarters. She is trotting at quite a pace now, tracking the source of the stench. At night, it is always reassuring to see the moon shining through the branches overhead. The snowfall might have ceased, but the sky is clotted with winter clouds.

"Don't be scared," I whisper.

In response, Flori finds my hand. I take it without hesitation. I try not to question the wisdom of what we are doing out here now. I just keep telling myself that if I can clear up the mystery of the bad smell, then perhaps everything else will fall into place.

"Maybe there is nothing to fear," she says, only to pull up so abruptly that our fingers unclasp.

"What is it?" I ask in a whisper.

"*Listen.*"

Even Solace has stopped in her tracks. She stands with both ears twitching, holding her head upright. Then I hear it for myself. A crackling sound some way off. I shine my torch in the direction of the Squawk Box, but find I do not need the light.

"A bonfire," I whisper. "Do you see it through the trees? A bonfire is burning over there."

We continue along the path, scurrying now with our scarves still pressed to our noses. I hold Solace by her collar, reassured by the strength of the muscles moving beneath her coat. As we break from the path and approach the great twisted oak, I remember to pocket my head torch. There, under cover of darkness, we gather to peep around the trunk.

Just inside the chain-link fence, near the rabbit burrows, two men stand with their backs to us. Judging by their burly shoulders and shaven heads, I believe we are looking at Mister Petri's sons. They're facing the fire, and stoking it with sticks. A metal funnel hangs over the blaze. This feeds into a horizontal pipe that is bolted to the side of a silver bin beside the two men. Despite the lid, smoke is pouring out.

159

"How much longer?" one asks. "The old man has already torn strips off me for lighting the fire when there's no breeze to clear the stink."

"Any time now," his brother replies. "Salt-cured, fresh-smoked meat is on the order sheet, and that's what we'll be providing."

I turn to face Flori, and find she is already looking at me.

"Meat," she says. "All this time they've been smoking meat."

"But what meat stinks this bad?" I ask. "Could it be a sick rabbit? If they're smoking the remains of one that has exploded, I imagine it might smell dreadful!"

Flori turns her attention to the burrows, but not a bunny is in sight.

"Rabbits don't explode, Kamil. They *expire*, same as us."

"Then maybe they're smoking cuts of chicken," I suggest unconvincingly. "It would explain why we can't hear any hens."

Flori looks troubled as she strains to listen, and then utterly shocked when a ghastly screech rises over the poultry farm. It seems to go on for ever, and sounds like a million fingernails scraping down a blackboard. Solace fires up in response, until I grasp her muzzle.

"Oh my goodness..." Flori trails off as a single brilliant light pushes through the trees on the other side of the Squawk Box.

Solace strains to be released as the cause of the commotion approaches the main gates. She begins to bark, but nothing can be heard but the ear-piercing screech. I am so dumbstruck that I step out upon the path for a clearer view. At the same time, the two men hurry to detach the bin from the pipe. As they carry their prize towards the main buildings a piercing whistle cuts through the noise.

It can only have come from the giant that has just emerged from the tunnel.

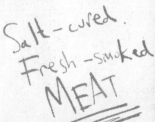

When the main gates open up, I believe I am witnessing something nobody ever thought would happen again. In a cloud of steam, with the squealing brakes easing now, a huge locomotive approaches the loading platform. With a slick black boiler, chrome running boards and a snowplough at the front that looks sharp as a butcher's blade, this train is as magnificent as it is menacing. A single freight carriage is coupled to this beast. In contrast to the engine, it is weather-beaten and rusting at the joints.

"Where has it come from?" asks Flori, sounding both spellbound and scared.

"If the Squawk Box really is rearing organic chickens," I suggest, "then perhaps it is here to make a collection."

As soon as the locomotive comes to a halt, the sliding door on the freight carriage opens up from the inside. Two boiler-suited figures climb out, clutching lanterns. With rubber gloves and boots, and face masks covering their mouths and noses, they jog through the steam and smoke now consuming the train. Its great headlamp floods the front of the slaughterhouse with white light, though the space inside is in darkness. The pair head straight for the building, and vanish into the gloom. Moments later, a dim glow pools from the entrance.

"That place is certainly *designed* to process poultry." Flori exchanges a glance with me. "But I still see no chickens."

As she speaks, the driver of the train climbs down the ladder from the cab. Immediately, a tall, strident fellow approaches with his hand outstretched.

"Mister Petri," I whisper.

"He looks very pleased with himself," observes Flori.

The two men greet one another like old friends. They converse for some time, laughing on occasion. Finally, the two boiler-suited figures struggle out of the slaughterhouse carrying a large shoulder of meat between them. It's been butchered and shrink-wrapped, but the shape and weight of it is clearly causing them some difficulty.

"What is that?" I ask. "Some kind of pork, or could it be beef?"

Flori doesn't answer straight away. Instead, we listen to Mister Petri yell at the two workers when one of them loses his grip and the meat hunk falls to the snow.

"Whatever it is must be very precious to him," she replies. "I've never seen him so quick-tempered."

With great care, the two men climb onto the loading platform and heave the shoulder into the freight carriage. Next they return to the slaughterhouse. After a moment, they appear once again carrying two more shrink-wrapped cuts.

"Do you recognize those?" I ask Flori, mindful that her father must have taught her how to skin and prepare all the wild game and deer he brought to the kitchen.

"Of course," she says. "That's a rack of ribs and some shin." Flori watches them load both into the carriage, and hurry back to the slaughterhouse once more. This time, they each come out with transparent plastic bags in both hands. "Here comes some heart, liver, some belly…" She pauses there for a moment. "It's very *meaty*, isn't it?"

"It certainly is," I say suspiciously. "For a chicken farm."

The bonfire spits and crackles just then. I return my attention to the blaze, and wonder just what kind of meat Mister Petri's sons have been smoking. Even with the scarf around my nose and mouth, the air is beginning to clear since they carried the bin away. I take a deep breath, only to expel it straight away as a dreadful thought enters my head.

166

In an instant, I feel the blood drain from me. My insides lurch and turn to stone. I even have to tell myself to inhale as best I can. I think back to what I had witnessed from the green. At the time I could not think why Mister Petri would want to spoil the largest lady in our community. Watching this scene unfold, in which great hunks of red meat have been carried out of the packing rooms, I can think of only one reason.

No chickens were being processed here, organic or otherwise. Could it be, I think to myself, that the meat just loaded onto the freight carriage was *human*?

"Cosmina," I say under my breath, feeling ever so faint all of a sudden. "Cosmina, what has become of you?"

"Beg pardon?" Flori does not take her eyes from the poultry farm.

"Nothing," I say, reeling. "Nothing at all."

I can barely take it in myself, let alone share such an unspeakable conclusion with my friend. We're on the far side of the woods after dark, with little power left in my head torch. If I tell Flori it would risk frightening the life out of her. More importantly, I have to be sure before I breathe a word.

"Now the train is preparing to leave." Flori tugs at my sleeve, drawing me from my thoughts. "What's the big hurry?"

When I look back, I see the locomotive and carriage revolving very slowly on the spot. My father had told me that the poultry farm was equipped with a mechanical turntable so the trains could be faced around for the return journey. I just never thought I would see it in action for myself.

Right now, I wish that had remained the case.

At one point, the huge headlamp sweeps over the huts and the bonfire. It then slices through the darkness, passing right across us. Flori shrinks away from it and I draw Solace back with me. Once the headlamp is shining through the woods to the black hole beyond, I see the two boiler-suited figures emerge from the slaughterhouse. This time, they seem quite comfortable with the neat gift boxes in their possession. I presume this must be the smoked cuts, which makes me feel sick to the pit of my stomach. Trading last instructions and farewells, they hop back inside the carriage. Finally, in a hiss of steam, the train begins its journey back the way it came.

Mister Petri stands beside the gates with both hands clasped behind his back, watching this mighty machine glide out into the night. His two sons join him just then, and clap him on the shoulders. As gates are closed and lamps extinguished, it seems we have stumbled upon a nocturnal job well done.

I turn to Flori. She is still watching, as if she cannot take her eyes away from what she has seen.

"Whatever has just been dispatched," she states darkly, "I am certain it is wrong."

In the days that follow,
as the snow clears along with the awful stink, I
return to the green with Solace, just before dawn
and as darkness falls. At first she complained and
pawed at the back door, but I have seen enough of
the woods for a while.

Instead, each time I throw sticks for my dog, I
focus on the cottage across from the great beech.
Cosmina's curtains remain closed, and her lamps
continue to burn, but I see no sign of her. Not one
silhouette at the window or sound of her trill voice.

Even her mobility scooter remains in exactly the same spot beside the door, reminding me of some dutiful steed.

Turned low, with a full load of oil and a nice long wick, some lamps can flicker for many days. It means there is only one way to find out if Cosmina is in residence, and that is to knock at her door. And yet every time I cross the green, a sense of dread grips me. I have no idea what I will do if she fails to answer. In some ways, I find it more bearable *not* knowing.

One other thing always encourages me to retreat. Old Wenzel's chickens. As soon as I approach Cosmina's cottage, they kick up a fuss from the other side of the fence. If she is feeding her face inside, I certainly see no evidence of it. And yet every time they squawk it unnerves me enough to walk away.

I try to peer over the fence, just to see what is going on, but as soon as I curl my fingers over the top the entire flock goes *bonkers*.

During this time, I do my very best to steer clear of Flori. Whenever I see her on the walk to and from the schoolhouse, I say nothing of my own suspicions. It is all so awful, I just cannot put it into words. What's more, in the light of day I find that her view of what we saw is beginning to soften. So instead of voicing my fears, I entertain her theory that Mister Petri might have gone quietly into the slaughter business.

"Maybe that train brought in livestock on an earlier run," she suggests. "Whether it's swine or cattle, the farm has the facilities to process almost anything. All the grinders and meat racks would only be rusting away up there, so it makes sense to put it to use. What I still don't understand is why he has to be so secretive."

Once again, poor Cosmina comes to my mind. Had I not already drawn my own conclusions, I might have accepted Flori's explanation. Instead, I find myself almost covering for Mister Petri. "It's a family affair," I say, even though this makes me all the more determined to uncover the truth. "If the community knew, there wouldn't be enough jobs to go round."

I am tempted to confide in Miss Milea. In class she continues to keep her bad hand hidden as best she can. Even so, there is an air of sadness about her that she cannot disguise. It is in her voice and in her eyes, which reminds me of my mother.

With nobody to share my fears, I find it hard to sleep. When I do drop off, deep into the night, it is not a pleasant place to be. In my nightmares, the faces I fear leer into the beam from my head torch. It isn't just Mister Petri and his sons, however. I dream of chickens, too, and when they come they're *everywhere*. A huge and noisy flock crammed inside my room. There they are, grubbing around on the floorboards, perched at the end of my bed and roosting in my cupboards, while the feathers in the air swirl and threaten to suffocate me. Sometimes it awakes me with a start, and reminds me I am quite alone in the dark. Then I am forced to lie awake, hoping a peaceful rest might come. That is when my thoughts turn to the tunnel, and what lies beyond.

We are all aware that wolves and bears roam the lowlands. We also know that outside the Grand Perimeter there is a strong chance of encountering those ragged escapees from the lunatic asylum. Because of this, the railway line remains quite a mystery. Nobody really knows where it goes. We can only imagine the faraway school canteens and

173

factories that the poultry farm once
supplied, though I do begin to wonder
if they are enclosed communities just
as we are.

Come the night before Mister
Petri is due to hand out the
weekly provisions, this is
all I think about.

For I cannot sleep a wink.

# 32

I arrive in line having skipped breakfast. This morning, I have no stomach for anything. I see Flori in the queue ahead of me, as well as Miss Milea. I even have a clear view of Mister Petri. He is handing out parcels with vigour today, while his sons stand sentry as if they expect us to start a riot. I just wish that Cosmina was present, but she is nowhere to be seen.

"*There you are! Enjoy! There's a little extra to go round for everyone this week. Don't let any go to waste!*"

Every time I step forward, the more nervous I become. Watching Miss Milea depart and then Flori, my heart begins to beat like a trapped bird.

With Mister Petri boasting that we are all in for a treat, I cannot help thinking that these extra tins, jars and cartons are going spare because of one less mouth to feed.

*"It's heartening to spoil you all for a change! As a community you have suffered great hardship, but I sense in the air that these lean times might soon be coming to an end!"*

As my turn approaches, I am foolish enough to catch his eye. In a blink, his expression switches from light to dark and then back to light again. It is nothing. Maybe just a momentary shrinking of his smile, but I have to force myself to stay where I am. If I leave the queue now, we will go hungry for seven long days.

*"Is your mother well? I trust she is eating a square meal a day?"*

A moment passes before I realize Mister Petri is addressing me. I stir from my thoughts with a start, and find my turn has come. Stepping up to the back of the truck, I clear my throat and speak.

"My mother is fine," I say nervously. "She is in need of a little direction and encouragement sometimes, but thank you for your concern."

Mister Petri is looking down at me with his hands on his hips. As ever, he's wearing a shirt with rolled-up sleeves and braces, with an apron around his waist to protect his trousers. His only nod to the

fact that it is cold is the black silk scarf wrapped around his neck. From where I'm standing, I can see his nostrils flaring.

"I am pleased." Mister Petri considers me as he says this. Then he looks up over my head. "Tell me, have you seen Cosmina?"

Hearing him say her name aloud turns my spine to ice.

"Cosmina?" I try to sound surprised, and turn to look behind me. When I face back around he is regarding me once more. This time through narrowed eyes.

"It's most unlike her to be late. Would you be so good as to find out what has become of her?"

I open my mouth, squeak quietly, and then close it again.

"Me?" I say eventually. "Why me?"

Mister Petri frowns, seemingly puzzled by my response.

"Because I asked you politely," he says, with just a hint of menace in his voice. Before I have time to step away, he chuckles teasingly and hands me a food parcel. "Deliver this to her cottage, and when you come back I'll slip a few more tins into your parcel. Consider it a reward for running this little errand."

I gaze at him, replaying in my head what he has just said.

"Very well." I step out of the queue, still looking at him as I retreat, seeking some sign that he is fooling with me. Mister Petri makes a little circling gesture with his finger. Obediently, I turn for the cottage.

As I approach Cosmina's door, the flock of chickens over the fence strike up once again. I hesitate, but only for a moment. I am sure that Mister Petri is still watching me. Even if he is serving the queue, I don't doubt that he'll have one eye on my progress.

"He knows what has become of her," I say to myself. "This parcel won't bring her back."

With one clammy hand, I clasp the knocker and rap it three times against the door.

"Hullo? Cosmina…? I have your weekly provisions."

There is no response.

I try one more time, raising my voice to be heard over the noise from the chickens. This close to the window, even with the curtains drawn, I note that a lamp is still flickering inside. As I wait, I turn nervously to find Mister Petri watching me, as are many left in the line. All of a sudden, I do not know whether I should try one more time or give up and face him again. I am torn by indecision, and so caught up in my thoughts that I jump on hearing my own name.

"Kamil? Is that you? If that is you, Kamil, perhaps you would be so kind as to let yourself in through the back door."

"Cosmina?" I am so surprised that I repeat myself. "Cosmina?"

"The back door, boy. The door at the back of the cottage!"

It isn't just Mister Petri who watches me skirt around the cottage. Now I have the attention of *everyone* in the queue. Cosmina called out quietly, but the noise from Wenzel's chickens has caused all heads to turn. As I skirt out of sight, the volume from the other side of the fence rises even higher. Still, I am relieved that I cannot be seen now. At the same time, I am concerned for Cosmina. Unusually, her shrill tone of voice has gone. She sounds somewhat small. Embarrassed, even.

"*Are you alone, Kamil?*" she calls to me from inside. "*I trust you're alone?*"

I reach the back door and try the handle. I enter the cottage, but what I find makes me step back in surprise.

"What has happened here?"

Before me, filling the door frame from the kitchen, I find the figure behind the voice. Cosmina Barbescu grunts at me, and cranes her neck like a tortoise.

"I'm stuck," she says. "I am stuck and I cannot get out!"

My first thought is that she is alive, but not so well. For Cosmina appears to be quite jammed. She struggles to free herself, but her huge body is just too big to shift one way or the other.

"How long have you been like this?" I ask, trying to make sense of the situation.

"Days," she howls in defeat. "Days and nights!"

Cosmina Barbescu is wearing a nightgown, slippers, a shawl and her horn-rimmed spectacles. I grasp her upper arm, trying hard not to think about the way her flesh folds around my fingers, and tug gently.

She does not budge from the door frame.

"I'll have to get help," I tell her.

"*No!* The shame of it!" She gestures at the food parcel at my feet. "Mister Petri always packs

182

a jar of lard in there for me. It's greasy stuff, Kamil. Very greasy indeed."

I am so shocked by the jam Cosmina is in that I only now feel some relief at having found her at all. As I rummage through the provisions to find the jar, I question what it was I had witnessed at the poultry farm. If I believed Mister Petri had moved into the slaughter business, this suggested I was very much mistaken.

"Here it is." Removing the lid from the jar, I scoop out a curl of the waxy gloop with my fingertips. Hesitantly, I stand and face Cosmina. She is still heaving away, teeth gritted, desperate to be free, and so I tell her to relax.

"How can I?" she pants. "I am stuck fast in a doorway, Kamil. Trapped like a rabbit in a snare!"

I take a deep breath. Then, hiding my disgust, I attempt to ease my fingertips between the frame and the fleshy figure squashed into it. I work from her armpit down, prodding in the lard with my fingertips and returning to the pot several times. Eventually, with each side of the frame greased, I take her upper arm once more.

"When I pull," I tell her, bracing myself now, "you push."

This time, I am not so gentle. I heave as hard as I can. At the same time, Cosmina makes every effort to haul herself free. First her eyes pinch, then her cheeks turn red, and finally her entire face starts to quiver with the effort.

"Put your back into it!" she urges as I take both wrists and dig my heels in hard. "If I don't eat soon I might fade away!"

At this, a splintering sound creeps into our puffs and grunting. It spreads so quickly that I do not have time to react and get clear. All I hear is timber and masonry giving way, upon which a startled-looking Cosmina travels towards me.

"Oh no!" I throw my hands in front of me, only to be flattened by a very great weight indeed.

On the floor, in darkness, I feel as if I am suffocating under a mattress. I try to push Cosmina off, but have to wait for her to stop spluttering and struggle to her feet.

"Thank goodness, Kamil! Thank goodness for you!"

We stand, with some effort, and inspect the damage. In place of the door frame is a ragged hole in the brickwork.

"I blame this cold weather," she says. "The cold has shrunk the door frame timbers. I can't think how else I could have become stuck like that."

I begin to dust myself down, but choose not to point out the obvious.

# 34

On my return to the truck, I find everyone has collected their provisions for the week except me.

"How is she?" Mister Petri is waiting with my parcel in his hands. "I trust you found her in good health?"

"Cosmina was very grateful to me," I tell him, having sworn not to breathe a word to anyone about how I had found her. "Though dare I say, I think you may be spoiling her just a little too much?"

I only utter such rash words because I am no longer as petrified of the poultry farm owner as I was before I knocked on Cosmina's door. He may not be the butcher I had feared him to be, but it still seems wrong to encourage a woman of her size to keep piling on the pounds.

When is my lunar calendar?

Mister Petri seems affronted by my comment. He glances at his sons, as if to check he has heard me correctly, and then returns his gaze to mine.

"*Everyone* in the community has extra rations this week," he reminds me with a frown. "For once, there is *more* than enough to go round." He reaches down to hand me my parcel. Without a doubt, it feels a little heavier than usual. Then, clasping his chin between his thumb and forefinger, he steps back to consider me. Once again I feel uncomfortable in his presence. It doesn't help that his two sons are regarding me without a hint of good humour. After a moment, Mister Petri turns to his shelves at the rear of the truck. When he comes back, I see two tins of peaches in syrup in hand.

"Maybe I should listen to you," he says, sounding more pleasant all of a sudden. He even leaves me with a smile, adding both tins to my parcel. "You've earned this today, Kamil. Spoil *yourself*!"

On the way home, I pass Cosmina's cottage. The curtains are open now and I can see her clearly in the kitchen. She is at her table, in the same night-dress as when I found her, hungrily spooning down the contents of a tin from her provisions.

I only draw to a halt on walking by the neighbouring shack. Old Wenzel's place has always been a little run-down, but right now it seems quite neglected.

Leaves have blown across the steps to his front door, while a large cobweb spans the porch. Had it not been for the cacophony struck up by the chickens in his yard, I might have passed on by. At first I think his flock are protesting at Cosmina's eating habits, but as I walk on the din becomes more intense. It's enough to bring me to a stop once more.

I dare to glance back at the truck. Mister Petri and his sons are paying no attention to me now. They're climbing into the cab, preparing to move off. I cannot ignore this level of clucking and flapping, so I wait for the truck to pull away and then duck under the cobweb to knock on Wenzel's door. The front windows are thick with grime and all I can see is bare furniture in shadow. More immediately, my presence here on his stoop has caused his poultry to go *berserk*. Not only are they squawking, I can hear them crashing from one side of the yard to the other. When I cross to the corner of the shack and peer towards the yard gate, I even see a flurry of downy feathers blow up into the air.

"What *is* up with you?" I ask, and decide to investigate for myself.

As soon as I creak open the gate, I can see straight away that it is not Cosmina who concerns these birds. Looking at them now, I realize they have been desperately trying to draw attention to *themselves*. The chickens in our community might be noted for their scrawniness, but this has gone too far.

"You poor souls," I declare, spotting the empty hopper. "Why has Wenzel not been feeding you?"

I cross the yard and immediately find myself surrounded by swarming hens. Some are so starved that they peck desperately at my ankles. Gritting my teeth, I collect the hopper and fill it from the sack of pellets I find inside Wenzel's shed. As soon as I set it down for them, the flock abandon me for their feed, which leaves me to return my attention to the shack.

At first, I do not think about why the back door is hanging from one hinge. I am so shocked by what I have found in the yard that a moment passes before I realize that it must have been opened by force.

"Wenzel?" Dropping my provisions, I steel myself to venture inside. *"Wenzel?"*

A few days would pass before
everyone accepted that the old man
really had gone missing. To begin
with, the community gossips held the
view that he had taken himself into the
woods or even climbed the mountain scarp
to enjoy some peace and quiet. Wenzel had
never been one for company, after all, so at first
his disappearance was not met with much sense of
urgency.

It is during school hours that I watch the first
search party fan across the meadow. Throughout
the lesson I pray they will see fit to investigate the
poultry farm. I might have been wrong in suspecting

that Mister Petri had dispatched Cosmina Barbescu, but now I am convinced he is behind old Wenzel's disappearance. I only have to think back to the night I witnessed him feeding Cosmina. I was so caught up in what I could see through her kitchen window that I failed to consider what his sons were doing. I feel certain this is when they took the old man away. I do not wish to think about his fate, but the vile smell that crept out of the woods the next morning tells me more than I need to know.

"Please pay attention, Kamil." I turn from the window to find Miss Milea addressing me. "We are all hoping they will find Wenzel," she tells me, "but it is important that you focus on your studies."

"Yes, Miss."

Something has happened to my teacher. She has changed in so many ways. It isn't just her finger that has gone missing since she ventured into that building inside the Squawk Box. Everything from her pretty smile to her sunny nature has vanished, too. Between lessons, when I tried to share with her my suspicions about Mister Petri and the activity I had seen at the farm, she just looked haunted. Then when I explained my conviction that he was behind old Wenzel's disappearance, Miss Milea simply closed her eyes, pinched the bridge of her nose and asked for a moment to herself.

Even Flori refuses to believe me. On the way home from school, having seen the search party return from the woods empty-handed, she simply suggests that I keep such accusations to myself.

"You'll be for it if Mister Petri hears that you've been saying he took Wenzel for his meat. How can you say such a thing, Kamil? And who on earth would buy it? The market for chickens might have changed, but I cannot believe that people have developed a taste for human flesh!"

"Then where is old Wenzel?" I stop and face her. Flori drops her gaze from mine. "What is it?" I ask.

She looks back at me once more. "It is an awful thought, Kamil, but perhaps you should ask yourself the same thing about your father."

"No." I take a step away, reeling from her suggestion. "That would be *unthinkable*!"

That evening, I feel as if Flori has sown a seed in my mind that refuses to lie dormant. Despite myself, it grows and spreads and flourishes much stronger than any crop we might have planted on the green. Had Mister Petri claimed my father? The poacher had certainly suggested the poultry farm owner knew more than he had let on about his disappearance, but could such an atrocity be true?

I lie on my bed and stare at the ceiling. With evidence that he had transformed the Squawk Box into some kind of human abattoir, there would be *uproar* in the community. On the shelf beside me stand two tins of peaches in syrup. I just cannot bring myself to eat them.

I can hear my mother downstairs. She is talking to Solace, telling her to be patient. I know that my dog must be exercised. Before I join them, I peel back my curtain and peer outside. Missing just the slightest of bites, the moon has almost completed her cycle amidst a swirl of stars. The cobbles and the rooftops shine with this nocturne light, while the scarp overlooking our community could be foiled in silver.

All is quiet. Stillness prevails. The perfect night, I decide in my current frame of mind, for a walk in the woods.

## 36

Solace halts at the mouth
of the path, expecting me
to turn around. I walk on
by with my head torch fully
charged. Of course I am
scared, alone out here after
dark. But I am also determined to shine a light on
the scene of a crime that
has eaten into our lives.

I follow the path
at a brisk pace. Moon-
beams drop through the
branches and boughs,

illuminating the undergrowth. Several times I disturb a bird or small animal, but the sound of scurrying and flapping does not halt me. I stop only when I reach the twisted oak. There, I pocket my torch, catch my breath and peer out from behind the trunk.

I had spotted the floodlights some way back, looming through the trees. It is the first time I have ever seen them in operation. I am surprised that they have been switched on at all, in view of what has been going on here. Somehow it leaves me feeling that the Squawk Box is slowly coming alive again. Once she is running at full tilt, I fear that nothing will be able to stop her.

The compound is bathed in a harsh artificial glare, forcing shadows from the buildings and the hopper to reach out in four directions. Outside the fence, I note rabbits grazing. In the moonlight, some seem larger than others. They also seem more nervous, as if perhaps they know what is in store for them. Most notable of all is the red and white cordon tape that has been strung on skewed, makeshift posts around the entire clearing. If Mister Petri arranged this to scare me away, it will not work. He can cook up

195

1st angel X

2nd angel X

as many stories as he
likes about infection
spreading through the
warrens underground.
In my heart, I know that
I have returned to the
scene of an atrocity. If only
I could prove it.

I scan the space inside
the chain-link fence,
seeking some sign of life.
The tick and hum of the
generator cuts the silence, but
that is all. It seems strange, compared with
the industrious activity I had witnessed here with
Flori.

As I look around, I note that Solace is rooting
about in the undergrowth. If anyone else were
here, my dog would huff and growl. The Squawk
Box might be deserted, yet I can't help sensing she
is ready to open her gates at any time. Everything
seems so *prepared*.

+1 = 3

3 + 3 + 3 = 9

Sept → X

I am so lost in thought that when the meteor sails
across the night sky over the clearing I don't quite
take it in.

At first I hear a crackle and a whoosh, and then
suddenly there it is, blazing overhead.

196

*"Look!"* I cry at Solace, but already she is barking and bouncing up onto her hind legs as if to see it off. "Isn't it beautiful?"

It is the first falling star that I have ever seen. Just two other members of the community have claimed to witness one over the years, and now my time has come. I am amazed at how gracefully it passes, burning like a lamp and showering a trail of sparks in its wake. It has come in over the mountain scarp, and now disappears from sight in the direction of the lowlands.

Immediately, Solace falls quiet. I listen for the sound of an impact, but hear only the hum of the generator once again.

Despite my excitement at such an unexpected and August spectacle, I am aware that I have used up much of the energy in my head torch. So I turn for home with Solace, who lopes ahead of me. As I follow her towards the trees, I feel elated by what I have seen. I plan to tell Flori at school the next day, but then something else comes to my attention. Something I really do not wish to see.

"Oh no," I say under my breath. "Not again."

Solace is the first to discover it, planted squarely

197

in the ground where the path snakes into the woods. I sprint to catch up, note her breath has turned to vapour, and pull her away from what she has found.

Another raven. Another dead bird with chicken skulls twined to its back. Not four this time, but three.

Without a doubt, the whole gruesome piece has been left here for me. Both wings hang limp in the moon-light. One of them appears broken. I look around briefly, but see no sign of life. What I do feel is a deathly chill, just as I did the last time. My mouth is dry and I feel like I want to cry. It is a most horrible thing, but I cannot drag my eyes away. Indeed, the skulls appear to be gazing directly at me. This time, I think I understand what they're trying to say.

"What have we done to deserve this?" I ask, as if in response to what has come into my head. "Why can't you leave us alone?"

## 37

"Three more people shall be taken from us. They will simply be spirited away from our community, just like poor old Wenzel."

When I share this with Flori the next day, she just looks puzzled.

"You seem very sure," she says. "How do you know?"

I tell her about what I had found in the woods. If the ravens that had been left for us represented darkness and death, as Flori's father had said, then the message they carried was now crystal clear.

"Don't you see? Each skull represents a person! Wenzel is gone, so now there are three skulls left. And if the bird signifies the season as well as the

*the divisibility of three*

*Why?*

199

fate in store for these poor souls, then we face a very bleak winter indeed."

We are talking in Flori's yard. At our feet, dozens of chickens are merrily milling about. In Wenzel's absence, her father has adopted his flock. I'd helped him to marshal them through the lanes to their cottage. This proved to be a much easier task than we had thought. Ever since I found them in such a desperate state, they'd taken quite a shine to me. Just now, for example, when I called upon Flori, they scuttled up to greet me. If I wasn't here with such sinister news, I would have found them quite delightful.

"So who will be next?" asks Flori, sounding a little anxious.

I rake a hand through my hair and clasp the nape of my neck. "Cosmina worries me desperately. I am certain that Mister Petri has designs on her. He has to be feeding her up for a reason."

Flori turns her attention to the chickens. It is as if she cannot bear to hold my eye because she fears that I am right. "And after Cosmina," she asks, only to gasp and meet my gaze once more, "could it be *us*?"

"It could be anyone," I assure her, even if the thought does unsettle me.

Flori dwells on what I have said for a moment. "Even if I believe you," she says next, "everybody else will dismiss your claims out of hand. We don't even know who is planting these ghastly messages for us."

As she says this, I cannot help but turn my attention to the figure at work in the woodshed. Flori's father is at his bench, preparing a trap. When I look back at her, I realize with a jolt that she knows what I am thinking.

"No way," she says, scowling now. "If my father wished for us to steer clear of the poultry farm he would simply tell us to our faces. Why would he resort to such scare tactics? He is a good man, Kamil, as well you know."

I cannot counter this. If anything, I am just frustrated that I cannot turn to an adult for help. By speaking up, I would risk being considered a nuisance. If anyone complained to my mother, and she forbade me from interfering in Mister Petri's business, it would only leave him free to carry out more diabolical acts. I did not think I could live with that, which is why I had put together a plan of action.

"Whoever is behind the warnings," I tell her, "the important thing is that we find a way to make sure nobody else goes missing."

"How?"

I flatten my lips and prepare to tell her.

"After dark, Cosmina Barbescu must not be allowed to leave our sight. I believe she is quite safe

201

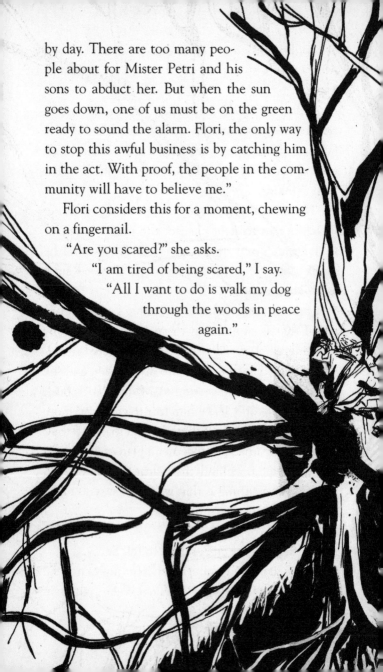

by day. There are too many people about for Mister Petri and his
sons to abduct her. But when the sun
goes down, one of us must be on the green
ready to sound the alarm. Flori, the only way
to stop this awful business is by catching him
in the act. With proof, the people in the community will have to believe me."

Flori considers this for a moment, chewing
on a fingernail.

"Are you scared?" she asks.

"I am tired of being scared," I say.

"All I want to do is walk my dog
through the woods in peace
again."

## 38

That night, as a harsh frost settles over the green, I question whether I am doing the right thing. I am wearing my warmest coat, hat, scarf and gloves, but the cold pinches my fingertips and my toes. I decided I should leave Solace at home, for fear that she might bark and give me away. It leaves me feeling vulnerable, but I cannot give up. Not while Mister Petri stands over Cosmina in her kitchen and spoon-feeds her yet more treats.

*"Now this, my lovely, is a rich and buttery goose foie gras flavoured with truffles... What do you make of it? Taste good?"*

*"Exquisite!"*

*"Then try a little more. This time, I'll just place a little dollop of onion jam on the top."*

Listening to their conversation has left me feeling queasy. I am hungry, but would have no appetite for food so rich and unusual. Nor could I manage the amount Cosmina has consumed. It began not long after I climbed into the tree. Mister Petri had pulled up, alone in his truck, and transported a huge hamper to her door. I heard some surprise and then amusement in his voice on entering her cottage, and put this down to the collapsed kitchen door frame. A minute later, their silhouettes cast against the curtains told me that the feeding had started.

Now, as Cosmina refuses a third helping of fattened goose liver, it seems she might at last be full. I sit up on the branch I am straddling, and wait for Mister Petri to appear at the front door. As I do so, a clucking sound draws my attention to the grass below. There, zigzagging towards the foot of the tree, I am confronted by the sight of one of old Wenzel's chickens. She looks up, shakes her feathers through, and chatters at me.

"Shh!" I press a finger to my lips. "Go home!"

Cocking her head, the hen catches my eye. She holds my gaze, blinking curiously. I have no idea what she is doing here at this hour. What is clear is that she has overcome her instinctive fear of being pounced upon and eaten after dark. I just cannot fathom why she would run such a risk.

*"Cosmina, may I say what a pleasure it is to keep company with someone who truly understands the delights of fine cuisine."*

I hold my breath as Mister Petri emerges. Behind him, Cosmina looks bigger than ever. I judge that she could fit through the front door, but not for much longer, and wonder whether the poultry farm owner has been struck by the same thought. He kisses her hand with a flourish, and encourages her to retire to bed.

"I shall certainly sleep soundly," she says. "Without old Wenzel next door, I will not have to suffer the indignity of him shouting at me from his bedroom window with accusations of snoring."

Mister Petri spreads his hands wide. "Then something good has come from this tragedy. Indeed, with one less mouth to feed, every member of this community can enjoy extra tins, jars and cartons in their weekly parcel."

"Why, you make it sound like we should *welcome* his disappearance!"

"I dare say there is cause for quiet celebration."

I watch the pair laughing heart-
ily at this. If Cosmina knew that I
could hear such cruel humour, I like
to think she would be ashamed at
herself. Even the chicken below me
seems upset by their presence. She
crosses back and forth in front of
the tree, clucking pointedly in the
direction of the cottage.

"Can I expect to dine with you
again soon?" asks Cosmina as Mister
Petri climbs into his cab.

"Oh, very soon," he replies, and fires
up the engine. "Very soon indeed."

The next three nights followed the same pattern. Mister Petri would arrive with a hamper crammed with food, and then leave with it empty. Every time he drove away into the darkness, I would wait for Cosmina Barbescu to extinguish the lamps in her cottage before heading home to thaw out.

The only thing to differ from one night to the next was the number of chickens who joined me.

The first night, having swung down from the tree, I found myself talking to the hen at my feet.

"So, my feathered friend," I said, breathing warm air into my cupped hands, "is it time we tucked up for the night?"

At this, the chicken turned a circle and then followed me through the lanes. At my gate, I watched her bouncing happily towards Flori's cottage, where she hopped the fence to join her sleeping sisters in their coop.

The next evening, the chicken returned with one of her number in tow. She too displayed hostility towards Mister Petri once he had climbed into the cab of his truck and driven into the night. Had he glanced in his rear-view mirror, he would actually have seen her giving chase. Her pursuit did not last long before she returned to the tree, where I questioned them both about their behaviour.

"What has got into you, girls?" I asked. "You do not have to concern yourselves with me. I can take care of myself."

On the third night, after several counts from my hiding place in the branches, I calculated that every single one of Wenzel's old flock had gathered beneath me. When Mister Petri made his exit from the cottage, they created enough noise to momentarily draw his attention. Mercifully, none of them broke out of the darkness until he had pulled off in his truck.

Now, on the fourth night since assuming my post,

I find myself joined not just by Wenzel's flock but by the poacher's poultry, too. While Mister Petri feeds Cosmina, they keep their clucking to a low level. With what feels like an army of chickens below me, my concern is how they will respond when he reappears at the front door. For an hour at least I fret about this, and even consider heading home early to draw them away. I only have to think about what might happen in my absence, however, to persuade myself to stay put. So focused am I on the feeding taking place behind the closed door that I'm startled when a figure appears below, causing the flock to divide.

"Kamil," says Flori, peering up at me, "why have you brought all these chickens? Are they your friends now?"

I am pleased to see her, but urge her to keep quiet and join me up in the branches. "We cannot afford to be spotted," I whisper.

"These hens aren't helping."

"I didn't encourage them to come!" I protest as she hauls herself up. "They've just started following me here."

Flori settles on a branch beside me. She peers across at the cottage. Judging by the silhouettes, Mister Petri is hand-feeding Cosmina once more. I cannot work out what it is, but every spoonful that he sweeps from can to mouth slops across the table.

209

"How long has she been eating?" asks Flori.

"A couple of hours," I say, yawning to myself. "He'll be finished soon."

She looks across at me. "Why don't you let me take over this evening? If there's any funny business I'll raise the alarm."

"I'm fine," I tell her.

"Go to bed, Kamil. You look so tired."

"Cosmina must be close to bursting. I fear it will not be long before Mister Petri pounces."

"He can try," she replies, "but I will scream like a banshee if he does. I guarantee that within seconds half the community will be out of their beds and peering from their windows."

I smile to myself, and decide that perhaps I should catch up on some sleep. "Thank you for joining me, Flori."

"We're in this together," she says. "Whatever happens."

I clamber from my branch, into a pool of chickens.

"I'll see you tomorrow in class," I say, and turn to leave. As I do so, I hear Flori giggle. I know why, and sense my cheeks flush. For with every step I take, the hens fall in behind, and follow me home across the green.

The next morning, on returning from the meadow with Solace, I cannot get to my door for poultry.

At a time when they should be on the lay, I discover the flock outside my cottage, grubbing happily in the first few bars of light. Even without counting, I wonder whether I am looking at every single hen in this community.

"Hello?" I say, with some surprise. "Next thing you'll be asking to come inside."

As soon as they see my dog they clear a path for us. I open my front door gingerly. Solace slips through, and I follow quickly behind, but it seems I am wrong about their intentions. The hens simply

watch us enter, and then return to the work of seeking out seeds and snails and bugs to eat.

My mother is at the table, nursing a cup of mint
tea. "They began to arrive a few minutes ago," she
says. "Most odd."

I sit down for my breakfast.
In front of me is a bowl of
steaming porridge. The
milk may have come
powdered, but with
hot water it is tasty
enough. This week

we have enjoyed a wider range of choice in our food parcel. I know the reason why, of course, but do not wish to dwell on that now.

"Are you eating?" I ask between mouthfuls.

My mother appears to search her thoughts before answering. "Oh," she declares, as if the very idea of food had left her head entirely. "Yes, I probably should."

For a long time I have worried about her strength. Lately, it seems to me that I should also be concerned about her mind. She has become so wrapped up in her memories that nothing else seems to matter. Looking at her now, I wonder how different she would be had my father still been here to eat with us. It is not something I can ponder for long, and so I hurry to scrape my bowl clean and tell her I must leave for school.

"Please look after yourself," I say. "For my sake as well as yours."

Outside, on stepping into the low winter sun, all the chickens turn their attention to me. I pause, adjust the school bag around my shoulder, and feel suddenly outnumbered.

"Ladies," I say with a nod. "May I pass?"

Hesitantly, I take one step forward. Sure enough,

to my relief, the hens in front of me cluck and retreat a little. Picking up the pace, I find my path is unobstructed as they fan apart. As I advance, however, they promptly regroup in my wake. At the gate I spin around without warning, startling those bravest of the birds who have crept up behind me.

"I'm going to school," I say, almost snapping at them now. "Please don't follow me. You don't belong there. My classmates will laugh at me."

As soon as I take to my seat, Miss Milea asks me if I am responsible for the poultry crammed into the courtyard.

"This is a place of learning," she says over the sniggers. "It is *not* a poultry farm."

My teacher is alone in not finding this amusing. If anything, she seems quite troubled at the sight of so many hens hemmed in on four sides.

"I'm sorry," I say, quite genuinely. "I'm hoping that if I ignore them they'll go away."

Flori is sitting beside me. She swaps me a look, and shakes her head in disbelief. "What have you done to deserve their attention?" she asks under her breath. "Every time I look in their eyes I think they know something about you."

"They won't stay all day," I assure her. "Chickens are ruled by food. As soon as they get hungry, they'll head back to their yards and coops."

"Speaking of food," Flori adds quietly as Miss Milea begins the lesson, "Cosmina didn't stop eating until midnight. Mister Petri made sure she finished every crumb."

"It cannot go on," I say in a whisper. "Tonight we have to be prepared for the possibility that Mister Petri will attempt to take her away."

"He'll have to bring his sons," Flori points out. "There's no way that he alone could haul somebody so big into the back of his truck."

"Then we should be ready to raise the alarm together," I suggest.

As Flori agrees to this, the sound of Miss Milea's voice suddenly falls away. I sit up smartly to find her looking at me from her desk.

"Are you quite finished, Kamil?" she asks, in a way that makes me wonder if she heard every word I just said.

*Finish the story on an even page.*

# 41

Leaving the schoolhouse that afternoon, I try very hard to ignore the taunts. I am grateful to Flori for walking with me. I just wish the chickens would leave me alone. One glance over my shoulder confirms the flock are following me home.

"Maybe they're looking to you for protection," she suggests. "You saved old Wenzel's flock from starvation. Perhaps they feel that you hold the key to their future."

"All I know is that they aren't taking kindly to Mister Petri whenever he shows up."

"Can you blame them? All the hens in this community are escapees from his poultry farm. I imagine none of them consider him to be their friend."

"I don't believe Mister Petri has any further interest in chickens at all," I say. "I'm afraid his mind is on much meatier matters."

At home, with the hens left to poke about outside once again, I find my mother seated in the same chair I had left her in. She remains in her nightdress, with her white hair loose around her shoulders. Only one thing has changed. Seeing what it is leaves me beaming at her.

"I thought I would cook us both a nice supper," she says. "Wash your hands, Kamil, and then dine with me."

I do as I am told, and take to my chair. Like me, she gathers a knife and fork in hand, then tucks into the plate before her. We are eating a meal of steak and onion from the tin, canned potatoes and mushy peas. I am so pleased to see her enjoying her food that I barely glance at my own plate as I eat. It is only when we are both finished that I ask if she enjoyed it. My mother dabs her mouth with a napkin, and sits back in her chair.

"It was nice to eat as a family again," she says, and moves to collect her plate.

"Let me do that," I insist. "You sit by the wood burner and I'll wash the dishes."

My mother smiles and drifts from the kitchen. She looks frail and in need of a little guidance to get her through each day. Indeed, she has not questioned where I've been the past few nights. Despite this, in the lamplight she has some colour in her cheeks at last.

It is not just for this reason that I am feeling so spirited when I meet Flori under the beech tree. The fact that I have arrived without being trailed by chickens comes as some relief. I have Solace to thank for this. She had whined at me so pleadingly as I climbed into my coat that I felt bad about leaving her behind. Looking back, I wish that I had brought her with me every night.

"The entire flock stayed put," I say, patting my dog on the head. "As soon as they saw that Solace was accompanying me, they simply cleared a path for us."

Facing Solace now, I instruct her to stay out of sight. I look directly into her bottomless brown eyes when I say this. Sure enough, with a quiet whine of resignation, she slinks behind the trunk of the beech and settles between the roots there.

Tonight, wisps of cloud trail in front of the moon. She is at her fullest, shaped like a dinner plate, ready to be nibbled and gnawed away once more. It is crisp and chill, with a ground frost forming fast, which makes me wish I had my dog's thick winter coat. As we climb into the branches, our breath takes shape like fleeting phantoms.

"There she is," I say, focusing now on the rotund silhouette through the curtains. "She's setting the table."

"It can't be long," replies Flori.

"Poor Cosmina." I watch her laying out her knife and fork. "If she knew what Mister Petri was planning, she would flee for her life."

Flori arches one eyebrow and smiles. "Somehow I don't think it would be hard for him to catch up with her."

"Which is one more reason why we must sit tight," I say. "The people of this community must witness Mister Petri without his mask. They have to see for themselves the contempt in which he holds each and every one of us. Even if it means waiting until they have dragged her from her house, we cannot afford to let him get away with it again."

We both fall quiet at this. I hug myself inside my coat, anxious not to let the bitter cold overwhelm me.

A long time passes before we speak again. At one point Flori dozes off. I leave her to sleep for a while, then worry that she might stir and tumble to the ground. When I wake her she tells me she is fine, but soon her teeth are chattering.

"You should go home," I suggest. "Let Solace escort you. It's really very late."

"Not a chance. I'm staying."

My branch is wide enough for both of us to sit upon, and so I invite her to share my seat. Silently, with her eyes turned from mine, Flori accepts the offer. She settles close to me. A moment later, she inches a little nearer, and then rests her head against my chest.

I dare to fold my arm around her, and then throw all my concentration at the cottage. I can barely draw breath. I fear that if I speak my voice will emerge as a squeak. Within minutes Flori is asleep again. This time, I am content to leave her undisturbed. All I have to watch is Cosmina in her kitchen, but now I feel like I could sit here for ever. As time passes, I see her pacing sluggishly or sitting at the table with her chins in the palm of her hand. Throughout, I wonder if she'll ever give up and go to bed.

As I watch her drumming her fingers on the table, I hear the distant sound of chickens squabbling. Flori stirs and notes it, too. "What a fuss," she comments, stretching at the same time. "Something has really disturbed them."

"At this hour," I say, "they really should be tucked up inside their roosts…" There, my voice trails away. I had been about to mention how vulnerable hens are to night-time predators, only to be gripped by a sense of dread.

When Solace begins to huff and bark, I know exactly why.

"Mister Petri," I say with a gasp. "He's here!"

Flori casts her eye along the lane that flanks the green. "Where? I can't see him."

"The chickens!" is all I can think to reply, as I scramble to climb down from the tree. "They stayed away for a reason!"

# 42

My heart is racing on reaching my cottage. Flori is wide-eyed and breathless, though she has yet to catch up on the cause of my panic. At the gate, we find a sea of hens in a state of alarm. All of them are clucking and rearing up on flapping wings, but it is what

Page 222
X 3
?

I can see behind them that commands my attention.

The front door is wide open. Light from the wood burner plays across the kitchen.

My mother is nowhere to be seen.

"We're too late," I say. "Mister Petri has been and gone!"

Flori's mouth falls. She looks at me and then steps back, dropping her gaze at the same time.

"Look!" she says, pointing at the frosted cobbles. "Tyre marks!"

All the way here the chickens' behaviour had become clear to me. Tearing over the cobbles, I just knew why the flock had chosen to remain outside my cottage. In many ways Flori was right. These refugees from the poultry farm were wiser to the way its owner operated than we could ever hope to be. They hadn't stayed behind tonight because I had taken Solace with me. They had stood sentry for good reason. Of all the people in the community, I think to myself, Mr Petri hadn't picked on the largest individual.

He had targeted the most vulnerable.

I see Flori rush inside, and come to my senses. Following behind, I find her calling for my mother.

"It's no good," I howl. "She isn't here!"

"Oh, Kamil!"

Solace comes through the door now, pushing

between neighbours drawn from their beds. She sweeps the floor with her muzzle, and I know just whose scent my dog has picked up on as she begins to growl.

"I have to go." I turn to find Flori. "I must get to the Squawk Box as fast as I can!"

"Through the woods?" she asks.

"If it is quicker than travelling there by the service lane then perhaps I have a chance!"

I break away to grab my head torch, and then race for the back door.

Outside, I strap the torch on as I sprint into the night. A moment later, I hear a voice call my name behind me. I look around. With the lamplights in my cottage blazing, I see my dog making ground with Flori behind her.

"Thank you," I say, as she catches up with me. "There is no time to lose!"

Into the woods we run. Neither of us slows to adjust to the deepening darkness. With a frost on the floor and the moon behind us we race down what feels like an endless corridor of bare black trees. Once again, the glow from the distant flood-lights looms large through the branches. This time, I feel certain we will not find the Squawk Box abandoned.

Sure enough, as we throw ourselves behind the

trunk of the twisted oak, it is clear that tonight the place is a hive of activity. The same locomotive train stands at rest before the buffers with the rusting freight carriage in tow. Once more, its headlamp shines through blankets of steam. The entrance to the slaughterhouse stands open again, with the same eerie glow pooling from it.

"There's the truck!" I point out. It is parked beside the rail track buffers deep inside the courtyard. The rear door is open, but the vehicle is empty. Two workers cross the compound. Once more, they're wearing hooded boiler suits, with rubber boots, gloves, and masks to breathe through. One carries a bucket and a scrubbing brush. The other lugs a stack of metal baskets. Just then, two burly figures in butchers' aprons leave the foreman's office. They head for the slaughterhouse, carrying cleavers and saws. I recognize them immediately. With shaven heads on necks set low between their shoulders, we're looking at Mister Petri's sons.

"I can't watch!" Flori turns away as she says this. "I cannot bear to think what has happened, Kamil. I'm so sorry."

There is something in her voice that sounds so final. It's as if she believes there is nothing more we can do. But however bleak things seem, I will not give up on my mother like that.

"There might still be time." I break away from

the trunk, glancing back at Flori in the hope that she will join me, only to slam right into a figure in my path.

## 43

At once a pair of hands grip my upper arms.

"This is no place for you, Kamil." With a gasp I hear a female voice, and then breathe out in relief. Miss Milea is as startled as I am, but I cannot afford this hold-up. "I heard the commotion at your cottage. As soon as I arrived I knew that I would find you here."

"My mother is for the chop!" I say, close to tears. "I knew that I was right!"

Miss Milea's eyes widen. "You don't mean that." She clutches my wrists now. I can't help but stare at the stumps of her missing fingers. This time, she makes no effort to hide them. "Are you sure you're not mistaken?"

As she asks me this, I hear a cry die behind me.

"What is that?"

I break from Miss Milea to find Flori's attention directed at the burrows inside the cordon tape. Following her line of sight, I just glimpse a white cotton tail disappear down one of the rabbit holes. There is no opportunity for me to see if the bunny is swollen or bloated. A moment later, I hear a brief, muffled boom under the ground, and draw my own conclusion.

"You have to believe me," I implore them both. "I'm right about the rabbits and you just have to trust me about the Squawk Box. No chickens are being dispatched from here, organic or otherwise. That train is awaiting a very different cargo indeed!"

Miss Milea shifts her attention between us. From this vantage point, I spot Mister Petri approaching the locomotive. At the foot of the ladder, he appears to summon the train driver down from his cab. This time, instead of issuing a hearty welcome he gestures irritably at his wristwatch.

"The train is either early or late." Miss Milea takes a breath as the poultry farm owner turns and beckons another figure to join them. "It's arrived too soon," she confirms, with an air of relief. "The cargo is nowhere near ready."

It takes me a moment to realize that she's talking about the small, bewildered-looking figure that

Mister Petri has just beckoned over. I have to look twice before I absorb the fact that it is my mother. She is dressed in her nightclothes, with her white hair brushed for bed. Clutching at her sleeves as she walks out under the floodlights, she looks quite lost and alone.

"We have to save her," I say, just as Mister Petri's sons emerge from the slaughterhouse once more. They hang back from their father, but it's clear that they're ready for him now. Desperately, I turn to Miss Milea.

"I have all the proof I need that Mister Petri can be ruthless in his bid to keep people out of his poultry farm," she says, her gaze still locked on the man himself. "But if you are right, Kamil, then what he has been hiding beggars belief!"

At this, she snaps from her thoughts and faces me again. "How can I help?"

As I struggle to think, the two boiler-suited figures are next to emerge from the slaughterhouse. They head around the central hopper for the building closest to this side of the fence. It is here that we first saw Mister Petri's sons at work, and where Miss Milea had ventured with such gruesome consequences.

"The maintenance room," she says, sounding hollow all of a sudden. "They sharpen the blades in there."

Crouching together in the gloom now, we watch them enter the building. It's quite clear to me that scaling the chain-link fence would only invite their attention. So, I take in who I am looking at, and grasp at a plan.

"Listen," I say, drawing both Flori and Miss Milea about me. I even summon Solace should she stray and give us all away. "This is what I propose…"

# 44

Moments later,
when we break apart,
Flori catches my eye.

"Are you scared?" she asks.

"I cannot afford to be," I say in all honesty. "We must make every effort to rescue my mother."

With a grave expression, Miss Milea nods in support of what I have proposed.

"I know just what to do," she says. "And if you make it inside, I promise I will raise every living soul in our community and bring them to your assistance."

"Seek out my father first," says Flori. "If he knows what trouble we're about to be in he'll be here in no time."

As directed, my teacher withdraws,
taking Solace with her. Keeping to
the night-time shadows and the
undergrowth, the pair head around
the back end of the poultry farm.
At the same time, I set about
quietly removing a section of
the cordon tape surrounding

233

the clearing and wait for Flori to locate one of the snares she had set for the rabbits.

"Evidently I didn't make the loop big enough," she grumbles.

"You're lucky not to have a catch," I remind her, as she unearths the notched stake that kept the trigger wire sprung.

Flori gathers her materials and looks up at me. "I'm sorry I didn't believe you," she says. "For what it's worth, I got rid of the rabbit's paw when old Wenzel went missing. I thought it was bringing nothing but bad luck."

"Then let's hope our fortune changes," I reply, as we hurry for the tree that is central to our plan. We have picked this one for the sturdy bough hanging over the chain-link fence. Flori clasps her hands, offering me a foothold so I can climb into the branches. Once I am up there, with the cordon tape looped over my shoulder, I inch out along the bough. Passing over the fence, I feel totally exposed. All I can do is look back at Flori, and wait for her to give the signal.

After a moment, she cups her hands to her mouth and makes a hooting sound. Such is her skill, I could be listening to an owl.

Immediately, the sound of savage barking fills the air from the opposite side of the farm.

"Good girl," I say under my breath as Solace

obeys the instruction from our teacher to make a big, distracting noise. Sure enough, through the open door of the maintenance building, the two workers stop preparing their blades and turn to one another. Even Mister Petri breaks off his conversation with the train driver to look around, as do his sons.

With their attention drawn away, I continue to edge out along the tapering bough. My weight makes it bounce up and down, so it comes as some relief when I am told to secure one end of the cordon tape and drop the other end to the ground.

"Hurry," I hear Flori call. I am surprised to find her standing directly beneath me, on the inside of the chain-link fence. As the daughter of a poacher, it is clear to me that she has inherited her father's sense of stealth. "Swiftly now, Kamil."

With the tape knotted tightly round the branch, I retreat to the trunk of the tree. By the time I return to ground level, Solace has ceased barking and Flori has scrambled back to join me. Just inside the fence, I see she has reset the snare on the ground, but this time she has loosened up the loop as far as she can. She is holding the free end of the cordon tape, the plastic strip stretched taut. I trace it through the chain-link fence, then through the snare, to where it is anchored to the ground by the notched stake. Flori has pulled it so tight that the tip of the bound branch is almost touching the stake. Should she release the tape, the branch would snap upwards and all hell break loose underneath.

"Are we ready?" I ask.

Mister Petri has stepped back from the train driver. The two workers in the maintenance hut have returned to sharpening their blades. It is a task marked by the rhythmic scrape of steel on whetstone. Right now I know that Solace will be guiding Miss Milea back through the woods to our community. Even so, there is no way she can raise help in time to stop the worst from happening.

"The trap is set," replies Flori.

"Now we just need to bait it," I say, and take the tape from her.

*"Hey, over here!"*

Flori has to repeat herself before the figures in the building hear her. They turn, and seem both surprised and alarmed to find anyone out in the clearing at night. Flori shines my head torch up into her face and waves at them. Immediately, the two men set down their tools and step out of the building. I am crouching in the gloom beside her, with the tape clutched tight in my grasp. Watching them advance, I fix my attention on the snare and brace myself for their arrival. I even begin to count their footfalls.

"Girl, you had better start running now—"

I release the tape just as soon as the two men

plant their feet inside the loop. The end leaves my
hand and whistles through the chain-link fence. In
a blink, with a deep swooping sound, the branch
springs upwards. It drags the snare tight
around their ankles, hauling them high into
the air. The clonk as their heads connect
with the branch makes me wince, but it
leaves them dazed and groaning. And
that gives us the break we need.

"Let's go!" With a gesture at the two
figures dangling from the branch, Flori
urges me to scale the chain-link fence
with her. "We need to strip
them of their boiler
suits before they come
round. Take their boots, masks,
*everything*! The disguise will give us
access to the slaughterhouse."

"And then what?" I ask,
fearful of what I might find.

At the summit of the
fence, we have a clear view
of the locomotive. The
driver now stands alone at
the foot of the steps, checking the watch attached
to his breast pocket. I look towards the slaughterhouse and catch my breath. For there is Mister
Petri, inviting my mother to step inside.

The boiler suits are too big for both of us. Even wearing them over our clothes, it's clear they are made for very big fellows indeed. We jam the legs into our rubber boots to keep them on our feet, and then snap on the masks and the gloves. Flori tosses the head torch back to me. The light is still glowing faintly as I pocket it, which I take to heart when we face each other. We may be well disguised, but there is no hiding the terror in her eyes. I have no doubt she can see it reflected in mine. Overhead, the two fellows we have snared dangle upside down, moaning in a daze.

"Are you ready?" I ask.

Without answer, and under the glare of the flood-lights, we set off towards the slaughterhouse.

As we approach the locomotive, it appears even bigger than I had realized. The wheels are huge, while the steam that drifts from between the great pistons makes me think of some dragon at rest. I catch the eye of the driver. He regards me from his cab. I look to my boots and hope the mask does not slip from my face.

At the slaughterhouse ramp, Flori taps me on the shoulder. I stop and face her.

"If we never make it out of here," she whispers, "I want you to know you're a very special friend to me."

"I'll do my best to make sure we all get out alive," I promise. "Even if it kills me."

The light in there seeps from a measly red bulb. I am also struck by how stiflingly hot it is as I creep inside. Keeping my head down, I slip behind a steel screen to the side. Flori follows close behind. There, I take a moment for my eyes to adjust.

"Chickens tend to be calm when the light is weak," she explains in a whisper. "Fooling them into believing it is sunset can help them feel more like they're heading for bed, when in fact—"

"I don't wish to think about that," I cut in, and peer out from behind the screen.

A central walkway leads through this long building, flanked by drains, scraping tables, scalding tubs and mincing machines. Overhead, an endless parade of meat hooks dangle motionless from a giant pulley circuit. Underneath, a familiar figure leads my poor mother towards the slaughter floor at the far end. There, half hidden by shadow in this grim light, Mister Petri's sons watch them approach. I see one of them tapping the flat side of his cleaver in the palm of his hand, and fear the worst is about to happen.

"We have to stop them!" I whisper urgently. "We must do *something*!"

Mister Petri escorts my mother with his arm

240

linked through hers. He is walking very slowly, stooping with every other step to avoid clipping his head on the hooks. He is also talking to her, I realize, and pointing things out as they pass the different sections. Without further thought, I join the walkway in a bid to get closer. Flori follows me. Together we try to look as much like the boiler-suited workers as we can. As I figure they are here to collect the final product, I grab a metal tray from a stack and deposit it on a steel-topped table. Flori mimics my action, even finding a cloth to polish them as I return for the others.

"So," I hear Mister Petri say, "once the chickens arrived here, they were knocked unconscious. We did this by applying an electric shock to the back of the head," he adds, as they pass a rack that holds a large metal wand with two prongs at one end. Mister Petri removes the wand from the rack. By way of demonstration, he triggers a fizzing blue bolt of electricity between the prongs. "Once they were out for the count, we strapped them onto the hooks and around they went. At each station stood a worker with a solitary task, which they'd execute in turn until the trays were packed with processed cuts and there was nothing but carcasses left on the hooks." He pauses there, makes the wand crackle one more time for his own amusement, and then returns it to the rack.

"That's quite an invention!" my mother remarks, sounding confused all the same.

"Indeed, your late husband was most impressed by many of my toys. The gristling machine interested him most of all," he says, gesturing at a wide hatch at the far end of the walkway. "You sling in any bits of birds that aren't fit for consumption, and the machine automatically grinds, dices and packages them into something that looks a little more palatable. When running a business like this," he finishes, "it's vital that *nothing* goes to waste."

Measure

My mother looks back at Mister Petri. The colour I had noticed in her cheeks earlier is now gone.

"I am most grateful to you for inviting me on this tour, Mister Petri. If you can manage to get the business up and running once again then you will certainly have my support. However, I really am quite tired. Would you take me home now?"

Mister Petri encourages her on towards the waiting butchers. "Oh, you're not just here by my invitation," he says. "This new venture is a *joint* undertaking."

I swap a glance with Flori, only for us both to melt further into the shadows when an all too familiar voice strikes up behind us.

## 46

*"Am I late? I do trust I am not too late!"*

Astride the mobility scooter my father had invented for her, with a lamp glowing inside her basket, Cosmina Barbescu rumbles up the ramp and into the slaughterhouse. Every bump causes shimmers to pass through her flabby arms and ankles.

"What is she doing here?" whispers Flori, having backed up against the table to let her through.

"The only way she could've driven from her cottage is by the service lane," I mutter under my breath. "And to do that she would need a key for the gates."

My suspicions rise further when Mister Petri greets her.

"You were right about our guest, my dear. She's been no trouble at all."

Peering through her horn-rimmed glasses, Cosmina Barbescu sizes up my mother.

"Well, there's not much on her, but she won't be missed," she says. "Just like old Wenzel himself."

Mister Petri beams at her. "Not just the elderly but the feeble and the miserable, eh? Some might find that unpalatable, Cosmina, but in these lean times we must do what we can."

"Indeed, Mister Petri. The demand may be for mature meat farmed from the older generations," she replies, "but it makes sense to pick off those who contribute least to the community. And if it means more provisions to go round, not to mention less tears and grumbling, then everyone is happy."

My mother listens to all this with her hand on her heart. I can see she is struggling to take it all in.

"Mister Petri," she says, "I really must insist that I go home now. My son will be wondering where I am."

"Ah, how *is* Kamil?" he asks, brightening all of a sudden. "Still throwing wild rumours about my affairs around the community? I'm rather hoping after this he'll realize that careless talk costs *lives*."

As he speaks, Flori collects the stack of trays. She crosses the walkway to a bank of levers and loads them onto a bench beside it. Turning to me, she

245

gestures at the pronged shock wand Mister Petri has now left behind. I glance back at Flori, and know just what she is asking me to do.

"Your son is a nuisance," adds Cosmina. "As soon as I spotted him hiding behind Mister Petri's truck recently, I knew we would have to find a way to frighten him away from our new business here."

"What business?" My mother looks both confused and frightened now. It's as if she's just waking up to the peril she is in.

With her life in my hands, I join the walkway once again. As casually as I can in my mask, boots and boiler suit, I snatch the shock wand from the rack.

"An *unspeakable* business!" I cry.

At once, Mister Petri and my mother look up with a start. Cosmina spins her mobility scooter around. When she sees me brandishing the wand, with Flori at my side, she seems utterly astonished.

I test the trigger. A bolt of electricity fizzes between the prongs. Such is the force, it makes both of us jump, but we cannot turn back now.

"A business that should never have begun," I stress, shaking in both fear and rage, and tearing the mask from my face. "Now let my mother go! She may be nothing more than meat to you, but she means an awful lot more to me."

Mister Petri is quick to recover his composure.

246

Any surprise in his eyes melts away when he grins at me. "Good evening, Kamil. I thought I heard your hound barking a little earlier. It's no surprise to think you'd be snooping around my property once again, although I underestimated your stupidity. I really didn't believe you would dare to come this far."

As Mister Petri speaks, his sons move in behind him from the shadows of the slaughter floor.

247

"Please," I say. "Just let my mother go."

"That's exactly what we intend," he replies. "Once she's been processed, we'll pack her off by rail and expect a healthy return for our product."

Just hearing him say this leaves me struggling to find the right words. "What has possessed you to be so wicked?" I ask eventually.

"We live in lean times," he says with a shrug. "We are all desperate in our own way."

"Maybe so," I say, "but turning on each other goes against nature itself!"

Mister Petri looks increasingly uncomfortable as I speak. I even sense that he is ashamed of the operation we have uncovered.

"I must confess, I've only recently become aware of the demand for human meat," he says, shifting on his feet now. "It's very much a niche market, but nonetheless the price per kilogram makes it all worthwhile."

I am disgusted by what I hear. "How did you know such a market even exists?"

"I hear things," he says. "My train driver makes many stops in his line of work, and forges valuable contacts. Had it not been for your father, in fact, the Squawk Box might still be producing eggs and processing chickens. At the time, in order to stay in business, all I asked was that he invent a way for me to pack in more poultry. Sadly, he refused. He claimed it would be inhumane, and argued that I should go *organic*."

organ – ic

Cosmina chuckles when he says this, as if the very notion is a joke. Even Mister Petri brightens up. "In some ways, we *are* organic now. Old Wenzel was free to roam," he tells me, and then drops all sign of humour, "and so too was your father."

I tighten my grip on the shock wand so much that my knuckles turn white. "You killed him," I confirm in a whisper. "You killed him and you processed him."

Mister Petri spreads his hands. "It was an unhappy accident. Our discussion about the future of the farm had become a little heated. At one point, I admit, I may have shoved him in frustration. The poor man simply tripped and banged his head. It didn't look good for him, Kamil, and, well, it was a chance to test the market, I suppose…"

As he trails off, my mother sobs and tries to struggle from his grip on her. Flori simply shakes her head.

"How can one man do such a thing to another?" she asks.

"It's an acquired taste," says Cosmina, in a way that makes me wonder whether she herself has tried it. "Mature meat is very much in flavour this season. You don't want to serve up anything too fatty, of course – lean cuts are the most tender. Now be a good boy, Kamil, and put down that wand."

"Only when you release my mother," I say, shaking my head.

Cosmina Barbescu repeats my appeal in a mocking voice, and then shifts her gearstick into drive. With a shudder, the mobility scooter moves towards us.

"Drop the wand," she growls, "or I'll flatten you!"

# 47

I back away as this humming mass of wheels and flesh bears down upon me. I know I could just turn and flee from the slaughterhouse, but I cannot leave my mother. Flori retreats alongside me. Desperately, we look around. Another step backwards and we draw level with the table where we had first breathed in so Cosmina could pass. Twisting around, I see the stack of trays that Flori had placed on the bench, then lock my gaze upon the bank of levers beside it. Holding out hope that rust has not set into the system, I reach out and pull the biggest lever of all.

"What are you doing?" Cosmina comes to a halt, distracted by the rattle and clang of chains pulling tight. Behind her, as the meat hooks overhead sway into life, it is Mister Petri who looks most alarmed of all. Abandoning my mother, and being sure to duck as the first hook creaks by, he orders his sons to act.

"Make them pay!" he yells over the noise of the pulley chains. "And make it *painful*!"

Seeing both sons loom from the shadows with their cleavers and saws is enough to stir me into action. Cosmina turns in her seat, urging the two butchers to hurry as I scramble over her mobility scooter with the electric wand in hand and hurl myself at Mister Petri. The prongs connect with his backside in a shower of sparks, and with a yelp his heels leave the walkway. He twists around to face me, his eyes bulging and his mouth a perfect circle, just as a meat hook scythes towards him.

"Watch out!" I say, but it's too late. The hook snares his shirt collar, and scoops him off his feet. "You too, Cosmina!"

As Mister Petri is dragged towards her by the

rotating pulley system, Cosmina Barbescu manages to shift her great body just out of his path. Helplessly, the poultry farm owner is hauled over her mobility scooter. He struggles to lock a shoe around the steering column, only to kick back hard on the gearstick. As the hook drags him onwards, Cosmina finds her mobility scooter heading in the opposite direction. I see her grasp the gearstick, but the scooter continues to wheel backwards.

"It's jammed!" she screeches, moving much faster in reverse than she had done crawling forward. "You've broken it!"

I step out of the way as she passes, and draw my mother close to me. Amidst the clunking of the pulley system, Mister Petri continues to bellow for assistance. He travels towards the front of the slaughterhouse, flailing uselessly from the meat hook as his sons look on, dumbstruck. Flori glances at me, and I see a glint in her eye. Without word, she reaches for the lever beside the one I had pulled and hauls that down as well. In response, the pulley system speeds up by a gear.

"Let me off!" cries Mister Petri, with his hands around the hook now. "Boys, get me down from here!"

This time, Flori doesn't just slam down one more lever. She works every single control in the row. By the time she has finished, Mister Petri is swooping down the back straight like a wrecking ball. Swinging wide into the walkway, he narrowly misses Cosmina and knifes between his two sons. This time, without a second glance at us, they make an effort to chase after him.

Such is the spectacle, along with the deafening noise, that Cosmina only returns to my mind when I hear her shriek and call my name. I turn to see the mobility scooter at the far end of the slaughterhouse, now just feet from the gristling machine.

"Help *me* first!" she yells, and stretches both arms in my direction.

Immediately, I leave my mother and rush to her assistance. Even as I move, she is framed by an ominous black hole in which blades rotate in a blur. I sprint towards her, but the distance is just too great. The scooter's rear wheels sink into the guttering and thud against the wall. As the vehicle tips, I see Cosmina thrown back. I think at first she will stop herself, but such is her weight that she just rolls off like an overstuffed rag doll into the dark maw behind her.

Instinctively, I turn away and cover my ears. The scream is very brief – unlike the persistent roar Mister Petri is making as he wheels around.

"Grab me on the way round!" he yells to his sons across the slaughterhouse floor. "Your weight should rip my collar free!"

I race back to Flori and my mother. "We have to get out of here," Flori cries over the noise, and gestures towards the door. "But those goons are blocking the way!"

"This time, boys! I'm coming around…"

Mister Petri is hurtling towards his sons. They're standing on the walkway as ordered, braced to grab their father as he passes between them. As soon as they make contact, the chains groan with their additional weight, but the speed does not drop at all. Instead, with two big fellows clinging to his legs, I hear the sound of shredding fabric.

"That isn't his collar!" Flori cries. "It's his trousers!"

"Never mind that," I say, with my attention fixed on the open entrance. "Let's go!"

Together, we hurry back along the walkway. My mother struggles to keep our pace, but Flori and I support her between us. Just as I inform her that help is on the way, however, shadows fall across the entrance.

When I find myself facing two large figures in their socks and underpants, I know they are not just here for their boiler suits. The pair don't look so dazed any more. At first they seem quite taken aback at what they've encountered here, then both turn their eyes on us and scowl.

Before I can act, my mother steps forward from between us. "Just hold it right there!" she yells over the din of the pulleys. "Have you gentlemen really thought this through?"

I have never heard her speak so forcefully. It makes her sound quite alive.

"You should know that as I speak the alarm is being raised in our community," she continues. "At any time now, you can expect a mob to spill through those doors, and they will not take kindly to what they see here!"

Flori also listens with an air of surprise and admiration, before her attention turns to a whirring noise that joins the sound of the pulleys overhead.

"What's that?" She points at a wall-mounted conveyor belt that spans the length of the slaughterhouse. It's just begun to move, and a file of small, marbled pink cubes is now parading towards a collection cage near the entrance. "Oh."

Immediately, I see why she is lost for words. For the belt originates from a hatch beside the gristling machine. If this is Cosmina coming out, I wonder if the cubes will ever stop.

Just then, Mister Petri and his sons swing around in front of the gristler. As they're swept along the length of the walkway, it is clear to one and all that the fabric of his trousers will not hold out for much longer.

"Get off!" he cries, attempting to shake free from his sons now. "You'll bring us all down!"

My mother sees them coming, and quickly returns to addressing the two men at the entrance. "I strongly suggest you cut your losses and climb back on that train now," she says. "You can take those cubes with you. We have no use or desire for them here. Whatever fiends savour human flesh will find more than enough for them there."

For a moment, we are met with baleful glares. "What more do you want?" she reasons, as Mister Petri and his flailing sons bear down behind us. "Be gone from our community. Step aside and leave us in peace!"

For one dreadful moment, the two half-naked workers look set to stand fast. Then, with an air of sheepishness and shame, they do as my mother has asked. Immediately we rush from the walkway, scrambling to be clear of the revolving trio.

"Switch it off!" demands Mister Petri with unbridled fury as they wheel by. "And will you boys *do* as you are told?"

He struggles to lose his two hefty offspring as they head for the rear of the slaughterhouse, but each time he kicks, his trousers continue to rip. I want to call out that he's risking life and limb should any of them slip within range of the gristling machine. It is Flori who has other ideas.

"Let's get away," she says. "I don't want to be here for a moment longer."

We hurry outside, and don't look back when the shredding we can hear is matched by mortal cries. We keep on moving even when that sound crunches into silence.

Outside, under the stars on this frost-bound night, I see the train driver looking very anxious indeed. He's leaning out from his cab, straining to see what's going on, and seems aghast on laying eyes on us.

Just then the two men whose boiler suits we had borrowed scramble out from the slaughterhouse. They're each carrying a haul of cubes in their arms, which they rush to load onto the carriage. When they hurry back for more, we simply step out of their path. The driver watches all this with an air of panic. It clearly gets the better of him, because he then rushes down the ladder to operate the mechanical turning circle himself. A minute later, facing in the right direction, the locomotive grinds into life. His two return passengers have to hurl their second batch of cubes into the moving carriage, followed by themselves.

The great headlamp penetrates deep between the trees. Briefly it lights up the vaulted brick walls inside the tunnel, before both the train and her awful freight glide on through. From the front gates of the poultry farm, we watch the tail lamps fade through the steam. I am so pleased to see this locomotive leaving, though I can't help thinking that it has been swallowed whole.

"We did it," I breathe, and hug my mother.

"What happened to your father is ghastly," she says, as together with Flori we make our way round to the burrows, "but at least we can be sure he rests in peace at last."

As we round the chain-link fence, I hear Solace barking in the distance. I also see lamps swaying towards us through the trees.

"What will they make of all this?" I wonder.

As I speak, a great white dog breaks from the approaching lamps, and rushes out under the moonlight.

"They will see a boy who has been to hell and back for his community," says Flori. "I hope this means they'll thank you."

261

To hell
and back

Solace bounds across the burrows. When I open my arms for her, she almost knocks me over. "I'm not so sure," I say, reaching to pet her. "What will happen to the weekly food provisions now?"

Nobody has a chance to respond. Not before a rough hand grabs me by the shoulder and hauls me from my dog. Solace snarls and snaps, but when a butcher's blade is pressed to my throat, Flori is quick to restrain her.

"There will be no more provisions," a voice hisses into my ear.

"Mister Petri!" I struggle to turn, but he holds me tight. Judging by the look of horror on my mother's face, I sense that he is in a bad way.

"You've made mincemeat of my sons and dear Cosmina," he continues, and begins to drag me backwards over the burrows. "I'll feed you to the same fate, and relish every moment!"

Solace growls and barks, but Mister Petri does not remove the blade from my throat. I fight to prise it away, but he has more strength than me. From the corner of my eye I see the poacher leading the way through the trees. With him are perhaps two dozen men and women from the community, including Miss Milea. Some carry hoes and pitchforks, but I fear that Mister Petri has the upper hand here. If he can make it inside the slaughterhouse, he'll only have to draw the bolt across the door and I'll end up leaving in boxes.

It is only when his foot sinks into a burrow that I seize the opportunity to slip from his grasp. I stumble as I do so, and drop to the ground. When I look back, I do not like what I see. Nor does Mister Petri.

He too is on his hands and knees. Unlike me, he's staring into the face of a grossly swollen bunny. This desperate beast has just emerged from the warren below, and draws gasps from Flori and my mother. With its front paws poking from a body like a barrel, the poor wretch is evidently on its last legs. It attempts to heave itself free, swelling before our eyes.

"Mister Petri, you should move away," I say, aware that the wretched rabbit's chest is as tight as the skin of a balloon. What's more, I can hear an ominous squeaking sound coming from inside it. I draw breath to urge him once again, only for the bunny to gasp in despair and burst at the seams.

As one we recoil from the blast. I throw my arm around my face and duck. When I look back, I see a man on his knees in defeat. With his fingertips, he wipes the gore from his eyes and cheeks. Next he spits out bits from his mouth. Clumps of fur are stuck to his neck and his shirt, but the look on his face is clear for all to see. After a moment to compose himself, he rises sombrely to his feet. His trousers are hanging in rags at the waist, just where his sons had been clinging.

"I'm finished with this place," he says. "It isn't safe to be here. Even if this sickness is confined to the rabbits for now, in time it will spread."

I think about how Flori had only touched the remains of a rabbit before falling sick. If she really had picked up something from it, then Mister Petri might be in much worse trouble having tasted such flesh in his mouth.

"Leave," my mother replies, and gestures at the mob approaching behind her. "Leave *now*."

He picks himself up, brushes down his shirt and turns to look in the direction of the railway track.

"You missed your train," I tell him. "Wherever you're heading, it's going to be a long and hazardous walk. In your shoes, I'd be afraid. As you've told us many times before, there are bears and wolves and lunatics at large beyond the Grand Perimeter."

"I'll survive," he says, and appears to hold a private smile in check. "Unlike your community, of course. Without me, you're finished."

"Without you, we have a chance!"

I hold his gaze and refuse to be the first to break it. Finally, with a strangely courteous bow, he turns and heads into the night.

As he leaves, I dwell upon the raven and the message that it carried. The four skulls bound to its back really had foretold how many people would not live to tell this tale. I'd simply failed to consider that Mister Petri's sons would join Cosmina and old Wenzel in that number.

As for who laid such omens in my path, I believe I will never know. But sure as I can be that my father walks with me in spirit, I would like to believe it was him.

Flori joins me now. She too is watching Mister Petri leave. It feels nice to have her close again.

"Is he going for good?"

I turn to see Miss Milea. I am pleased to see the figure beside her in the stalking coat, with ropes

266

and wire slung over his shoulder. The party she has mustered gather behind the poacher. Most have been called out in their nightclothes. Clutching their lamps and makeshift weapons, they seem both bewildered and alarmed.

"He won't be back," I say. "The Squawk Box belongs to the people now."

"But what kind of business can we run?" asks Miss Milea. "We don't stand a prayer's chance when all we have are hens. They cannot lay eggs that will hatch. And without chicks, we have no way of breeding them."

"We'll think of something," I reply, aware that the poacher is wisely using a stick to pick over the remains of the rabbit.

"No matter what business we begin," he says, "it must be small-scale and in harmony with the environment. It is no coincidence that the rabbits have picked up a disease so close to a poultry farm that went to such extremes."

"Are we in danger?" asks Flori.

The poacher unloads the snare wire from his shoulder. "We can clear the warrens and prepare for a fresh start," he says, and begins to set the first trap. "Just as we can with the Squawk Box."

The moon hangs over the scarp now, heading for the horizon. With a ground mist beginning to form around our feet, I realize we must be moving towards dawn. I plunge my hands in my pockets, feeling the chill out here, and find my head torch. It is dead, so I knock it against my palm a couple of times. My good fortune holds, because sure enough a dim glow builds. Just enough for me to see the way ahead.

"Where are you going?" asks Flori, as I call Solace to my side.

"I need to exercise my dog," I say, and head in the direction of the tunnel.

"But you've never gone that far," she calls, though I pretend not to hear her.

Sure enough, on reaching the rail track I hear the sound of a chainsaw striking up in the distance. I pause, listening to the same vicious buzz that begins whenever I venture this far, and then continue towards the tunnel.

"I'm not scared," I tell myself, for I am certain someone is watching over me. "I am scared of nothing at all!"

Solace pads ahead. She does not stop at the mouth of the tunnel and nor do I. Mister Petri has just trodden this path, but I have no intention of following in his footsteps all the way. I just want to see what it looks like on the other side. Even if I come face to face with the bears, the wolves or some bewildered soul in a straitjacket, I need to take it all in with my own eyes. By now the buzzing has built into a fury, but I am determined to put that behind me. With great relief, as I venture deeper, I find the sound of the chainsaw simply fades. In here the air is laced with the smell of coal smoke from the train. It is also very damp. My head torch is so weak that I can barely see my feet, but I will not stop now. I cannot turn around. So I crunch on over the ballast bed, mindful not to trip on the rails or the sleepers.

Eventually, after what seems like a lifetime, I see the faintest point of light ahead. I pick up the pace just a little, with Solace faithful at my side. As I draw closer to the end of the tunnel, it becomes clear that I am witnessing the very first fragments of the sunrise. Far across the lowlands, flanked by forest slopes, a first ray of light has broken. Now the buzz from the chainsaw has receded, I hear the distant clink of goat bells and a dawn chorus like no other. Among this glorious singing, I detect the sound of another bird. One that brings a thankful smile to my face.

"Solace," I say, "our prayers have been answered."

I see it at the mouth of the tunnel, scratching in the dirt. With not a single animal trap in view from here, it moves around quite freely. As yet more bars of light creep through the mist, I watch it hop up onto a rail and tip its head towards the horizon.

Finally, with the sunshine warming its fiery feathers, the cockerel crows with heart and soul to welcome this new day.

# Final Note

And so Kamil's world must come to a close, as indeed it will for us all at some time this year. Observant readers will now be wise to the precise date that a cataclysm like no other will befall us, which means my job is done.

It is a great pity that our days are likely to be numbered. I would dearly love to take this opportunity to introduce the next tale from my bunker. It is a story of a haunting like no other, but to tell you of the soul locked away at its heart would be pointless. Most of you will be gone, after all, unless you follow in my footsteps and make preparations for The End.

*Layla Strangelov*

# Acknowledgements

I should like to extend my appreciation to everyone involved in bringing my tales to light, whoever
you may be. Thanks in particular to Walker Books,
Philippa the fixer, and apologies to Matt Whyman.

Above all, I am indebted to a kind soul who has
allowed me to live life underground without want
for anything. Not least her ginger biscuits.

WWW.Strangolov.com

First published 2009 by Walker Books Ltd
87 Vauxhall Walk, London SE11 5HJ

2 4 6 8 10 9 7 5 3 1

Text © 2009 Lazlo Strangolov
Foreword © 2009 Matt Whyman
Illustrations © 2009 Quinton Winter

The right of Lazlo Strangolov and Quinton Winter to be identified as
author and illustrator respectively of this work has been asserted by
them in accordance with the Copyright, Designs and Patents Act 1988

This book has been typeset in Goudy Old Style

Printed in Italy by 🖨 Grafica Veneta S.p.A.

British Library Cataloguing in Publication Data:
a catalogue record for this book is available from the British Library

ISBN 978-1-4063-1660-5

www.walker.co.uk